BOOT HILL

Weston Clay

Curley Publishing, Inc.
South Yarmouth, Ma.

Library of Congress Cataloging-in-Publication Data

Clay, Weston.
  Boot Hill / Weston Clay.
    p. cm.
  1. Large type books. I. Title.
  [PS3553.L3854B66 1992]
  813'.54—dc20
  ISBN 0-7927-1227-7 (lg. print.)   91-27349
  ISBN 0-7927-0968-3 (lg. print: pbk.)   CIP

Copyright, 1950 by Phoenix Press

Published in Large Print by arrangement with Donald MacCampbell, Inc. in the United States, Canada, the U.K. and British Commonwealth and the rest of the world market.

Distributed in Great Britain, Ireland and the Commonwealth by CHIVERS LIBRARY SERVICES LIMITED, Bath BA1 3HB, England.

Printed in Great Britain

BOOT HILL

CHAPTER ONE

Sixteen-year-old Redman Paine looked at his two elder brothers enviously as Big Harry combed his rebellious, coal-black hair. Big Harry Westfall was one of the deadliest trigger slammers who ever operated along the Rio. He muttered, "Hold still now, Red," and tried to tame that cowlick that persisted in jumping up. Stringy Red Paine kept watching the husky Charlie and the handsome blond Hugo, his brothers, as they stood outside the door of the cabin arguing about who would ride the paint horse first. They were old enough so they didn't have to go to school anymore. Red Paine hoped he'd get that old soon.

"Hey, where's your necktie?" cried Big Harry.

"I don't want to wear one," Red Paine protested. "The other fellows don't."

"We don't care about the others. You're different. Go get your necktie afore I give you a licking," Big Harry ordered.

Red made a grimace but went into the corner room of the house he shared with his brothers and returned with a brown tie. Sometimes it seemed as if he were always

1

hearing that "you're different" thing. It was drilled into him repeatedly, as if he had to be better because he was an outlaw's son. Like giving the name of Paintor at school even though he knew his father's name was Paine.

Outside the door, the big-shouldered Charlie, almost as large as a full-grown man, was boasting that next year Dad was going to let him tote a gun. The slim Red smiled to himself as Big Harry laboriously knotted the tie at his collar. That was one of his secrets. Big Harry had been surreptitiously teaching him how to sling a Colts when the others weren't around. Even his father, Redman, Sr., didn't know about it. Big Harry gave him a whack on the back as he finished with the tie.

"All right, now, Little Red. And don't ride the daylights outa your pony down to the schoolhouse. You got plenty of time. Got all your books, now? How about that geography?"

It was then his father Big Red, came in from the kitchen, blowing on the tin cup of coffee he carried. "Red, what was this you were saying last night about the teacher asking what kind of business your father was in?"

Big Red hadn't been home when Little Red returned from school yesterday, hadn't come

2

in till late in the night, long after Red was in bed, in fact. Little Red had mentioned it to Harry and one of the other men.

Little Red said, "Mr. Brooks asked me again yesterday what kind of work my father did. Like you told me to tell him, I said you'd sold your ranch in the Mogolones before we came here. Then, in the afternoon, he asked me again – like – well, like he didn't believe me the first time."

Red saw the two older men exchange glances. He knew his father was an outlaw, a wanted man, the head of a bunch. That sometimes they moved quickly, suddenly, without much advance notice. That there were periods when he'd been boarded out with some family, when he didn't see his dad for weeks on end. But the thing in itself, the fact that his father was outside the Law, meant little to him. He knew his father as a gentle, kindly man, a man who told him stories in the long winter evenings when he was around, a man who read to him from the Bible after putting him to bed.

Harry Westfall said, "It's that bank shooting at Twin Forks, Red; that was bad. Folks were all riled up about it. There was no need to put lead in that old teller, Blair. And him having a younger brother who's a deputy makes things worse."

3

Big Red nodded. "I know. Well, I ran Gregory outa the bunch for doing it, didn't I? Shucks, we had what we went there for. The job was as good as done when he had to go trigger crazy."

"I warned you that Gregory was no danged good," Westfall said. "And now they're blaming you for the killing. Red, we oughta git out; we oughta git down south of the border for a spell. Things are going to get hotter up here. That's why they're asking the younker questions at school – it's the Blair killing. We know you didn't do it, but that doesn't help now."

Big Red ran a hand through his thinning hair. "I know; you're right, Harry. But there are no schools for the boy down south of the Line. Mebbe, in a few weeks. A boy needs education these days; I don't want him to grow up to be like me."

He patted Little Red's shoulder. "Don't worry, Red. Just tell 'em the story I already told you if they ask anything more. Just keep saying that. And – well, don't be afraid."

"I won't be afraid, Dad," Little Red said. Then he went out with Harry Westfall and mounted his pony beside the house. Harry straightened his necktie again. Red waved to his brothers, then rode the buckskin pony down the path from the house in the foothills,

4

down toward the trail that wound southward toward the schoolhouse out at the crossroads on the range.

Everything went all right till the recess at lunch hour, though Mr. Brooks, the teacher, did seem to be watching him surreptitiously at moments over the top of his glasses. Elmer Johnson, son of the owner of the big Box-J outfit, started it after they'd eaten their lunch in the yard. Red noticed him whispering with some of the other boys. Then the bigger Elmer, hands stuck in the pockets of his Levis, began to strut in front of the bench where Red sat.

"What does your father do, eh, Red?" he taunted. Red told him his dad was a retired rancher, but young Johnson kept asking it tauntingly. Then he suddenly used a new line. "Rancher, eh? Did he use his own or some other man's steers, hey?"

Little Red came off the bench, quivering, his hands balled into fists. Elmer Johnson, almost a head taller, laughed.

"What was the last jail your father was in, Red? And is Paintor your real handle, huh? Mebbe the Law is looking for your father, huh, Red?" He was just repeating some of the rumors he'd heard whispered about. "Mebbe your paw is hiding out, huh, Red? Mebbe he's scared!"

That last was too much. Despite young Johnson's superior size. Red went for him. They both swung wildly, then grappled. Then went down in the schoolyard, scrounging around in the dirt. The bigger Elmer had the better of it at first, pounding Red. Then, using a trick Harry Westfall had taught him a wrestling trick, Red got out from under and leaped up. Blood was running from a cut lip. Elmer got in a punch that knocked him down again, then stood there, laughing at him. Little Red shook his head to clear it, then clambered up off his hands and knees. He remembered something Harry had told him: that often you could whip a bigger man by coming back at him often enough. Some of those big fellows expected to win and their sand ran out if you kept coming back; and a heap of big men got hurt more easily than smaller determined hombres. He went back at Elmer Johnson again, with most of the other pupils yelling for Elmer.

Elmer sent him down into the dirt once more and tried to jump on him. But Little Red, spitting blood, rolled away. He regained his feet; when Elmer came at him that time, he ducked a swing, then landed a punch that sent the bigger boy back on his heels. Before he could recover, Red hit him another blow that sent him staggering back against the side

6

of the schoolhouse. Then Elmer Johnson lost his nerve, pulled a knife from inside his shirt, snapping open the blade.

It was only a big pocket knife, not a bowie. But the sight of it sent Redman Paine berserk. It seemed so completely unfair. He rushed Elmer before the latter could get his arm back for a thrust, got Elmer's knife hand. Again they went to the ground. But this time, Little Red was all over the cow king's son, twisting and pounding with his free hand. He wrested the knife from the now bawling Elmer's grip, was about to toss it aside and complete the job with his bare hands. Then a big adult hand had him by the back of his shirt collar. He was hauled to his feet to face Mr. Brooks.

"Bad blood will always tell!" the schoolteacher cried, striking the blade from Red's hand. "Like father, like son!"

Red tried to explain that it was Elmer Johnson's knife but the schoolteacher told him he didn't want to hear any of his lies. He hauled him inside and switched him about the legs with a switch he kept for that purpose, then made him sit in a back corner of the room for the rest of the afternoon. When the other pupils were dismissed, Red was kept an extra half-hour. He was still smarting inwardly at the injustice of it when he rode up the north trail on his pony. He was

7

determined to tell his father he wouldn't go to that school any more. Though he was still sore from it, it wasn't the switching itself that hurt as much as the idea his personal word had been spurned because he was the son of a suspicious man.

He came to the turn that led to the house in the foothills, and for the first time he noted a faint column of smoke from a dying fire. It was up where his home was. He rode on faster, his heart beating hard. Then he came around a clump of trees to the foot of the path and no house was there any more. What he saw seemed impossible at first: the smoldering charred skeleton of the place, the slow-smoking ashes where once it had stood. Right off, he sensed something worse had happened.

Tragedy stamped plain on his homely features, Harry Westfall came running down the path to him. "You're going to need a heap of nerve, younker," was the first thing big lumbering Harry said. Then, an arm wrapped around the boy's shoulders, Harry told him. His dad, Big Red, was dead, had been killed as he tried to stand off a posse that had come for him.

Little Red Paine, struggling against dry sobs that shook his body, was scarcely aware of the details then. Afterward he was to remember them. Harry had been away, had gone into town with Charlie and Hugo. The posse, led by Adam Blair, the deputy who was the young brother of the teller killed when the outfit had held up the bank at Twin Forks, had caught Red alone. From what Harry Westfall had learned of the story afterward, Redman Paine had been wounded right off but had refused to surrender when he heard they were charging him with the murder of the bank teller. Though innocent, he knew he'd never beat the charge in court. He had made a one-man stand.

When they set fire to the place, he had been driven into the open and cut down. There were three slugs in his chest beside the leg wound he had. The posse had already departed, two of them wounded in the siege; there had been sixteen altogether. When Little Red heard that, his chest went out a bit. They would have had to outnumber his father heavily to whip him, he told himself.

"Be brave, younker," Harry said heavily. "Your paw knew it would come this way – some day. On the owlhoot, we know."

Then he took him up to the mound behind the remnants of the house where he had already wrapped Big Red in a blanket and buried him. He'd made a rude cross fashioned of fresh-split wood for the head of the grave.

Charlie and Hugo were already there, the eldest, Charlie blubbering and raging at the same time. The blond Hugo stood very stiff and still, staring hard at the grave. Once he just muttered.

"Dad should've turned Gregory in. But he was too kind-hearted and figured how Gregory was a little locoed and just ran him down the trail. He should have turned him in. But he was too kind-hearted and said it would be double-crossing a poor devil who'd just lost his head. Dad was too kind-hearted." He didn't seem to be speaking to any of them. It was as if he were repeating a hard-learned lesson. "Dad was too kind-hearted."

Harry Westfall led them in a homemade prayer they repeated after him. The sun was already westering, filtering through the yellow pine on the slope. To Little Red, it seemed to throw a golden halo over the grave. He wanted to cry but wouldn't let himself. And it suddenly came to him that despite his youth and size, he was no longer "Little" Red; with his dad gone, he was Redman "Red" Paine.

The gunman finished his rude but sincere prayer and bent to brush a piece of charred paper from the house off the grave mound. They all said, "Amen." Harry replaced his sombrero.

"Your father was a fine gent, boys; never

forget that. And – and he died for something he didn't do. Big Red, he never shot no man that wasn't trying to get him. That's honest. And he was driven to the owlhoot in the very beginning for a shooting he had nothing to do with; he was innocent of that shooting like he was with this killing."

Big Charlie banged a fist into his other palm. "He was innocent. And when I'm a mite older and can really sling a gun, I'm coming back here and git that Adam Blair; by Gawd I swear it! They ordered us to quit the country, but some day I'm a-coming back. And I'll find every last man that was on that posse and I'll – I'll –" he broke off, emotion choking him.

"No, no you mustn't do that, Charlie," Harry Westfall said. There was almost a note of terror in his voice. "Big Red wouldn't have wanted that! Honest! You gotta promise, Charlie. Red didn't want any of you boys to be gunfighters. Once you git that stamp on you, you ain't got a chance any more. Red wanted you three to be inside the Law; you gotta promise, Charlie!"

"They killed him! I'll get revenge and –"

"No, Charlie," Westfall insisted, his own voice a little shaky with emotion. "He wouldn't want it that way. He used to say this would happen to him some day – that

11

they'd catch up with him. He was willing to take the chance, but Big Red didn't want for you boys to hit the owlhoot! You hear?"

Red, Little Red, couldn't stand it any more then. He almost thought he could see his dad with that crooked smile at the bottom of the grave. He could feel himself start to crack up inside. He ran for the trees. There amongst them he cried his bitter heart out, keeping from sight. But he made a solemn vow, even as he half strangled on his grief. He would grow up to be the man his father wanted him to be. He would be no owlhooter. He would have liked to swear vengeance as much as Charlie, but if his dad didn't want it that way, then it wouldn't be. Instead, he'd become somebody big and important, maybe a lawyer like his father used to talk of making him sometimes. . . .

CHAPTER TWO

That night they slept out on the trail after departing from the valley. Red was forced to ride double with Hugo. They only had the horses they sat on, the clothes they stood in, plus a few dollars Harry Westfall had in his pocket. He bought some grub for the trail with it in the morning. They talked over their plans.

Big Red had foreseen that this thing could happen. It would be the end of the bunch. The men had scattered for some weeks, anyway, following the bank holdup. But the father had given his instructions to Harry in case this should happen. Harry was to take them to a town called Endicott Flats where his dead wife's half-sister was married to a man named Groot, who had a general store there. Little Red didn't remember much of his mother who'd died shortly after his birth; he had never seen the so-called aunt over at Endicott Flats. Harry said Red had told him once he'd lent the wife's relatives some dinero to buy the store. It had never been repaid, so the Groots should be willing to take care of the boys till they could get on their feet.

"I'll be sending you some dinero to help out, too," Harry promised, wiping his mouth after the breakfast he'd cooked by the little creek.

The twenty-year old Charlie shook his head. "I don't want to go to any store. I aim to be a cowhand – for a spell, at least. I'll build me up a big herd; then we'll all be rich."

Westfall studied Charlie for some moments, then nodded, giving in. He said he reckoned

13

that could be arranged. He knew an old saddle pard who'd quit the owlhoot and gone straight and now had a small outfit up Big Steer Basin way. He'd probably give Charlie a job, seeing how big and strong he was. Charlie looked at his two brothers with a superior air. Red only wished he were old and strong enough to be a cowhand too. Somehow the Groots and their store didn't sound so good.

It was eight days later when they rode into Endicott Flats. Harry said that was good, because they were some distance from where they had just recently lived, even farther from the corner of the state where Big Red and his bunch used to ride. Folks down this way wouldn't have to know they were an outlaw's sons.

"And you're to behave like you ain't, too," Harry warned them again. "That's the way Red wanted for you to be brought up and to act."

They loped into the small settlement that was little more than a bump at the crosstrails where two stage lines passed. They found the store without trouble, a paint-peeling ramshackle building up from a yellow sluggish little creek. Red felt himself tighten inside as he eyed it. It seemed ready to totter on its foundations and it had an unkept,

14

unsuccessful air. Harry had sent a telegram on ahead from the first big town they'd hit after leaving their burnt-out home back in the valley. The Groots knew they were coming.

They entered the dim store, redolent of manila hemp and sorghum and smoked meat. There was also an odor of stale greasy cooking that young Red was going to come to hate. "Uncle" John Groot came out from behind a packing case at the rear, a stocky man with work-stooped shoulders and a sour bitter-thin mouth above an uneven black beard. He had beetling eyebrows and looked as if he'd long ago forgotten how to smile.

"I'm Harry Westfall," Westfall started to introduce them. "And these are —"

"Red Paine's brood, eh?" cut in Groot with a heavy unpleasant voice. There wasn't so much as a smile or a nod for the orphaned trio. He stared, then put down the hatchet he'd been working with, stepped to a doorway in the back partition, and called up a flight of unseen stairs, "Anna, they're here. Paine's boys, that we gotta take care of. They're here."

When "Aunt" Anna appeared, she was a fit counterpart for John Groot. She was skinny, with an equally hard mouth and cold staring eyes devoid of warmth or friendliness. She reminded Red of something that had withered

15

on the vine as she poked at the iron-gray wisps of hair that kept dangling down from beneath her sunbonnet. She nodded.

"They sure aren't very clean," she said finally.

Harry told her it was pretty hard to keep clean riding dusty trails for days on end. He kept patting Red and Hugo, the younger ones, behind the shoulders as if to brace them. He said Charlie wouldn't be staying.

Uncle John nodded, fingering his beard. "That's just as well; don't know how we could manage to feed three more mouths. Young uns eat a heap too. 'Cause, the two that are staying will have to do some work and help out around here."

"I'm not afraid to work," Red heard himself say clearly.

There wasn't much to it after that. Westfall wasn't asking to stay and split a bean. He and Charlie went out to the ponies. Red and Hugo stood beside them embarrassedly for a few moments. Then they shook hands all around. Charlie said:

"When I git my own spread, I'll send for you two. And it won't be as long as you think." He had been genuinely hurt by his father's sudden death, but he didn't show the marks of grief as plainly as his two brothers now. Charlie had always been rash

16

and impulsive, sure he was going to be a big potato some day. "I'll send for you, all right, boys."

Then he mounted, and he and Harry Westfall rode southward out of Endicott Flats.

"Hey, you two," called Groot from the doorway. "Shake a leg now. Got things for you to do. . . . This ain't like living around a camp. Honest folks got to work hard for a living!"

That was the way it was to be all the time. They worked with few lulls from the time they rose in the morning till the time they dropped onto their flimsy cots in the storeroom behind the store itself. There always seemed to be some chores; wood to cut, water to be carried, the store to be swept out. When they had nothing else to do Uncle John put them to cleaning up the yard in the rear. It was a litter of debris with piles of rusting tin cans and old packing boxes. It evidently hadn't been cleaned up in years.

After a couple of weeks, Groot picked up a few sway-backed old horses to operate a livery stable from the saddle-backing barn down by the creek, so they had the added task of keeping the barn clean and handling the ponies. The brothers wondered who used to do all the work before they came.

17

There was no break in the gruelling monotony of it except when the stagecoach came through pausing only a few minutes. Occasionally cowhands drifted in from the surrounding range instead of going into the big town of Alcord, but they spent practically all their time down in the settlement's lone barroom. The two boys were strictly barred from there by Uncle John, who considered even a single drink the curse of the Devil. He himself seldom spoke outside of giving orders, forever complaining about how the work was done and grunting about how poor business was.

Once Red mentioned school. There was one a few miles up the creek where there was another settlement. A circuit-riding schoolteacher visited there a few months of the year. Groot drew himself up as if the younker had asked for a thousand dollars.

"School? Are ye crazy boy? There ain't time for you to waste on reading and writin'! And if your paw hadn't wasted good dinero on such shennanigans, mebbe so now you wouldn't be objects of charity! *Sabe?*"

There was nothing more to be said, though Red colored with fury at the aspersion cast on his dad. They went on about their drab chores. At night there was another plain meal upstairs where Groot and his wife lived, with,

18

as always, never quite enough to eat. Uncle John said too much food made a man lazy. After, he'd sit with his greasy cards playing solitaire, sucking on his cold pipe. Hugo said he hated to refill it because he was always thinking of how much the tobacco cost. Aunt Anna sat in a creaking rocker, doing some sewing. All attempts at conversation were discouraged. Uncle John didn't believe in light talk.

Then there was a letter from Harry Westfall. It was to Red, strangely. It was postmarked from a town down near the Border. Harry said he was doing fairly well and that he was trying to get something fixed up so they could live together again. There was eight dollars in it, four for each of them.

Hugo fingered the four dollars out in the barn. "I wish I could get away from here," he said grimly. He was complaining a heap of late; he'd gotten into the trick of watching a departing stagecoach till it was gone from sight and there was just a bunch of dust over the trail where it had been.

Red didn't say anything. He didn't like it any better than Hugo did, but he was resolved to stick it out because his dad would have wanted them to. They had to grow up decent – not as trail bums. But it hurt him most when he had to go out in the settlement street in his ragged jeans with his knees poking through. Uncle John had new ones stacked on the shelves. But he claimed he couldn't afford to give them new ones yet.

About a week later, Red used his four dollars secretly. From the old saloon swamper who claimed to have been both an owlhooter and a deputy in his heyday, he bought a broken Frontier model Colts. The hammer was gone; it wouldn't shoot. But at least it gave him the chance to practice slinging a gun as Harry had taught him. The thoughtful Red had no intentions of becoming a gunfighter, but Harry had drilled into him that out here in the southwest an hombre had to know how to defend himself. "Like it says in the Bible," Harry had told him, "they's the quick and the dead. The quick are the ones who can sling a hogleg quick when they're forced to. And they stay alive."

And then there was a thing his dad had frequently said. Big Red claimed that no matter which side of the fence a man rode on he had to know how to stand on his own, single-handedly, when a clutch came. "A man's got to be true to his own self," was the way he put it. "A very famous writing fella, a Mr. Shakespeare, he said that once. Remember it, Son."

Red did. Whenever he got the chance

he slipped off into the brush by the cabin where the old swamper lived, dug the gun and the old belt and holster from a secret cache, strapped them on, then practiced the draw till his arm was ready to drop off. He practiced slinging the gun with both hands. He practiced the road agent's flip Harry Westfall had taught him, and the trick of putting a stone on the back of his outstretched shooting hand, then going for his weapon and seeing if he could fire before the stone hit the earth. Of course, he could only pretend he was firing.

It was about this time he began to dream of becoming a John Law. Then, when he was set with some way of supporting himself, why perhaps he could read law on the side and become a lawyer as his dad wished. His dad used to tell how Judge Talcombe down in the Strip had done that, coming up from a sheriff. His dad always said Talcombe was a fair man, too, administering justice without hate. Red went at his shooting practice again, making "bang-bang" noises to simulate actual firing.

When he got back to the store that afternoon, Hugo, who'd become introspective and taciturn, was livid, with a stormy look. Uncle John had struck him twice in the face, told him he had to be tamed because of the blood he sprang from. The words were what

21

made it so bad. Hugo's look grew grimmer as the day wore on.

That night, some extra sense brought Red suddenly wide awake on his cot in the drafty storeroom. There was no dark lump on Hugo's cot. But there was a piece of paper atop the blanket. Red took it over into the beam of moonlight from a high little window. It read:

Red, I'm leaving. I can't stand any more of it or I'd kill Groot some day. I'll try to find Charlie. Then we'll send for you. Just wait. Goodbye.

Hugo

Red caught his breath, suddenly assailed by a terrible loneliness. Then he let himself silently and cautiously out into the back yard, went down to the barn. It was as he feared. The blaze-faced old crowbait was missing; Hugo had stolen a horse.

CHAPTER THREE

John Groot went into a black rage when he discovered the missing boy and horse the next morning. He roared around for some time; then he suddenly dropped into silence and Red knew that was more dangerous. The man saddled up, said he was going into Alcord to report Hugo to the Law as a horse thief.

"And I'll go with the posse to hunt him down, too," he vowed. "There ain't no mercy in my heart for a criminal!"

John Groot was gone two days. During that time, Red lived in constant fear, with the woman refusing to speak to him except when necessary, sneering at him as if he were some kind of a sinner. Then Groot returned, trail-stained and dishevelled, pushing a limping pony. They had failed to find Hugo. Somehow he had made his getaway on that old crowbait. Red took a full breath for the first time.

It was about ten days later that a rider came through, leading the blaze-faced horse Hugo had actually borrowed, not stolen, as was proved now. He also had sent along a five-dollar bill for the use of the horse. Red felt almost like crying with relief.

The tag end of the summer faded fast. The wind whipping down from the pass in the northwest across the brown range grass began to carry a bit of it. And John Groot did two things. He gave Red a new pair of Levis and a used pair of his own boots. Red's toes were starting to come through his own. And Groot said:

"Boy, come next spring, mebbe we can send you to school."

Red figured he could somehow stand things then. He didn't realize it was an empty bribe, that Groot didn't want to lose another worker, to have him run off as his brother had.

The winter wore away. Work was harder than ever now, and that storeroom at the rear was unheated and icy cold. With his single thin blanket, Red shivered half the night. Then the last norther blanketed the range, half burying the settlement. No stages came through for over two days. There were reports of heavy losses in cattle trapped in the snow and cut off from their feed. Came the sudden thaw, with the whole landscape turned into mud as the warm winds and the strengthening sun ate away the snow. The few sprigs of green grass appeared. And the spring arrived. Uncle John kept putting off the schooling, talking of waiting till he could hire somebody to help him run the store.

It was then a girl came to visit in the settlement at the crossroads. Her name was Andrea Mason and she'd come to visit her aunt and uncle too. The latter ran the town's barroom. She was blond and very small and delicate. When he stood beside her for the first time, the black-haired Red realized how he'd begun to lengthen out. She liked him and his soft-spoken ways. It became customary each evening for him to go over and sit on the porch of her uncle's modest house with her.

Once she asked him what he wanted to become in life. He told her about his plans for wearing a lawman's badge and studying to be a regular lawyer after a spell. She shuddered at the idea of the danger in being a John Law, saying she was afraid of it. He looked at her blond daintiness, and allowed as how maybe he could forego that and finally get his own outfit as a cowman.

It was the next evening at sundown when he was talking to her at the gate of the yard that it happened. Three young fellows of the town came along, among them her cousin, Butch Mason, who already had a job as a cowhand with one of the spreads up to the north. They paused, stood whispering and chuckling together for a bit. Then the husky Butch pointed a mocking finger at the girl and began to tease her.

"Shame on Andrea for sparking with a danged lobo's son! Shame on Andrea, she goes with a no-good outlaw's boy!" he called.

Turning from the gate, Red felt himself go sheet white. For a few seconds, he surveyed the capering, jeering Butch, realizing the latter was older and bigger. Red Paine was never going to be as powerful or as tall as his father. He had rangy shoulders. But otherwise, he was as slim as a blade, a trifle short in the legs. Still, he knew he couldn't take those references to his dad.

"They made a cottonwood apple outa his paw, the outlaw!" taunted Butch Mason.

Red was on him, diving in like a lithe wildcat. The rugged Butch staggered Red with a couple of blows. But the lobo's son, darting and weaving, with lightning-swift hands, came smashing back, began to rock Butch Mason. The big fellow went down in the dust as Red simply swarmed over him. Even in the heat of the battle, he realized something then. It was more than blind temper that drove him when in a fight. It was some wilder thing, some instinctive knowledge that, because of what he was, he would have to be ready to beat down many a man in his life.

One of Butch's friends jumped in to his aid. But even with the bleeding Butch back on his feet and both of them punching at him, Red was beating them, battling like an untamed animal.

Then Old Man Mason the barroom owner came flying out of his house. Red's uncle, John Groot, came hurrying down the road from the store. Red was grabbed by the back of the neck and by the pants so he almost danced on air.

"You danged outlaw's son!" Groot roared. "You come along with me. I'll show ye, by grab!" He started Red up the road.

But not before the latter, despite a bleeding nose, got a look at Andrea, saw the shocked look on her face on learning that what Butch had called him was really so. He knew then that though he wasn't ashamed, he could never face her again.

John Groot dragged him back and into the storeroom. There, using a buckskin thong, he gave him a terrific lashing, panting out again and again, "You would get in a brawl with the son of one of my best customers!"

Red took the blows without whimper, even when they cut the shirt on his back. He was too proud to cry out, and he didn't fight back because he figured his uncle had the authority to do this just as his dad would have had. Finally it stopped. Groot threw the lash into a corner and then cuffed him a few times around the face.

"I've been too good to you, too easy," he puffed. "But things're going to change now! I'll learn ye! You're the son of an outlaw, a wild un! The son of a no-good skulking coyote, by grab! And if I have to break –"

27

Red Paine did hit him then, full in the mouth with his fist. Groot staggered back, then clutched at him. Red tore himself free, ducked away from the now berserk Groot's clutching hands. He would have been no match for the big man, but there was a barrel stave in the corner; grabbing it up, Red began to beat him over the head and the arms and the shoulders. Howling like a whipped coyote, Groot ran forward into the store, turning the key frantically in the connecting door from his side.

In the storeroom, Red let the stave drop with a futile gesture and stood quivering. After some minutes he went out into the dusk of the yard, plunged his head into the rain barrel. Then he headed out into the brush, knowing he would never return there again. He dug the broken useless gun out of the cache, half-circled around in the brush toward the other end of the town.

For a spell, he squatted as the night shadows thickened, speculating on finding Butch Mason and whaling the daylights out of him again. But then, with a maturity strange for one of his years, he realized Butch wasn't important, that he was only symbolic of what he might have to buck often till he proved himself a straight, square man, till he proved his strength. The important thing now was the

28

means of getting away.

Moving ahead till he could get a looksee at the main road, he was just in time to see a strange rider dropping down at the hitchrail of the barroom. The man had left his pony at one end near the alley running beside the place. The man went inside. And the wild plan began to evolve in the kid's hand. He would take that man's cayuse to get away on, but he would borrow it as Hugo had done John Groot's. He would return it. But to do that, he would have to learn who the jasper was, where to send the horse afterward.

Red edged out of the brush. Quick as an animal, he scurried across the road, then got into the dark alley with his broken gun. He began to sweat, shaking like an aspen. By peeking in a side window of Mason's place, he could pick out the strange rider at the bar, a barrel-chested gent with bushy tow hair. He was plump-faced but there was a certain hard-bitten note in every line of him. He had two more shots of whisky, then headed out. And the shaking inside Red Paine ceased. This was simply a nervy job that had to be done. And he would send the pony back soon.

The man came down the path, boots creaking, humming. Red moved like a ghost just as he got opposite the alley on the deserted street. He was out at his side in the gloom, the useless hogleg in the man's ribs almost before the other was aware of his presence.

"All right," Red said quietly but firmly. "Get into this alley, gopher! And the less noise – the less sorrow for you!"

They moved into the alley. Inside Mason's joint, a man laughed at a joke. Red spoke in a hurried whisper as the tow-headed one stood with hands half lifted.

"Look, I don't want your dinero. But I got to get quit of this pueblo pronto, so I'm going to borrow your horse. Tell me your handle and where to send it back later – as soon as I can – I will. I'm no horse thief. See?"

The man said, "You've done something here, button?"

Red nodded, "Never mind what. I got to pull stakes." He thought he heard somebody across the street, cut his eyes that way. "So I –"

It happened. The tow-headed one made two blinding fast moves with his half-lifted hands. He brought the left one down in a slicing movement that smashed Red Paine's wrist and his gun to one side. If he could have fired it then, he would only have shot at thin air. With his right hand, the jasper whipped a .32 from a shoulder hideout under his vest. He had it against Red's chest in the next moment.

30

It was a tough break. But to his own surprise, Red kept his head. He knew the next move in this game of guns, a risky one. But he had everything to lose if he were caught in an attempted holdup here. He said:

"All right, mister." He flipped his broken gun around by the trigger guard, extended it butt foremost to the other in a gesture of surrender, stepping backward half a pace.

The full-grown man reached for it with his left hand, lowering the right that held his .32. And then with an eye-defying speed, Red spun his gun draped from his index finger by the trigger guard. In a split-second, the butt was back in his hand and he'd rammed the muzzle deep into the tow-headed one's middle.

"I'm boss now," Red warned, voice a little cracked with strain. "No more tricks – or I blast!"

He had moved sideward so that the light from the side window of the whisky mill fell on his face. The tow-headed one blinked, then peered at him.

"The road agent's flip!" he gasped. "And I only saw one man who could handle a hogleg that dang fast! One!" He looked closer, then half smiled. Red had never realized that though he was much slimmer than his father, he had the same way of looking out of his gray

31

eyes, that he moved with the same effortless yet flashing grace. "Say, you wouldn't be Big Paine's button, would you?"

It was Red's turn to blink. "Why yes – I am."

The bigger one chuckled. "I used to know Big Red back in the old days. Come along, kid, I'll get you out of town. I got a pack animal with me you can ride."

A few moments later, they were riding off through the brush, avoiding either main trail for several hundred yards. Red Paine was putting Endicott Flats behind him forever, riding into a new life. . . .

CHAPTER FOUR

The man's name was Ed Chess, he said. He had a deep voice with a lazy way of speaking as if he were about to chuckle at any instant. He said he had known Big Red in the days when he rode the Cholla country. Red could remember those days because then he had gone to school at a place called Little Independence and lived in a boarding house that winter. Chess spoke highly of Big Red, saying he had never been afraid of anything mortal that walked. Chess admitted to having been in the rustling game back then.

Red was worried, despite the fact this man was helping him. He had to live up to what his dad wanted and not get tied in with an outlaw pack himself. He asked Ed Chess if he rode the owlhoot now.

"Naw, naw. With law and order cluttering up the whole country, it's too risky these days." He said he'd been in the Cherokee Strip when the U.S. marshals moved in to clean it up, that he'd been lucky to escape with his skin. "I'm in a right good business now. Tell you about it later." Red didn't press. He knew it was the unwritten courtesy of the trail not to ask too many questions. They rode southward in the night and went through a canyon to put the flatlands behind them. When they stopped to munch on some cold fried sow belly and Dutch oven bread, Red told him how things were at John Groot's place, how he had fled. Chess said that kind of a setup was no good, that he'd had good sense and nerve in getting out.

"I'll git you fixed up with something decent. Don't worry none. And let me tell you, I ain't never seen a slicker pelican at handling a gun." They bedded down then.

They rode for four days, rested most of the fifth. But that night, they covered a heap of

33

distance. Early the next morning, two miles on, they sighted a railroad line deep down in a cut in the hills that ran into the next town. Chess left Red at a creek up in the hills, saying it was better if he went into the town alone. "Your uncle might send word ahead an' claim you stole something, you know. He was an ornery old galoot."

Chess returned later in the afternoon. He said things were quiet enough down in the town, that he'd made some inquiries. Then he came out with a blue shirt and a pair of slightly worn leather batwing chaps for Red. They were a little bit on the big side, but he felt good when he donned them, no longer felt like some maverick dependent on some grudging distant relative's charity.

"I'll pay you for this rig soon as I find work," he told Ed Chess.

Chess passed it off with a wave. "Don't worry 'bout it. And don't worry about work. I'll get you a job at a real tophand's wages. Here."

What he handed over then was a cartridge belt with holster attached, then an ivory-handled .45 Colts. Chess grinned and said that one really fired, too. As he strapped on the belt and dug the hogleg into the holster, the slim Red choked up. He felt like a real man then. He saw Chess' eyes

34

lick with admiration as he practiced slinging the gun. Something in those eyes for that instant made Red wonder about Chess being an owlhooter again.

The older man seemed to read his mind. "Don't fret, button; I didn't steal 'em. And I'm a-going to git you a real job where you won't have to hide out, neither. . . . But first, I got a little personal business to tend to down in this pueblo. I can handle the thing myself all right. I got a score to settle. But – well, I'd like to know my back was covered when I was leaving."

After what this man had done for him, out of pure gratitude, Red had to agree to help. Chess said again it was a personal affair, that he meant to scare the daylights out of a couple of pelicans who'd gotten rough with him once. "I aim to collect some money owed me, you see."

They rode down out of hills into the town, crossing the railroad tracks. It was a large prosperous-looking place. Chess led the way down a side street that seemed jammed with honky tonks and gambling halls that were just swinging into life for the night. Down by a corner of a large dancehall, they dismounted, Red still riding the pack horse. Chess said:

"All right now, you stand close by this tree and keep watch on that front door. When I

35

come out, just chuck some lead if any snake tries to git me in the back. A wire-tough pack of homebrecitos hangs out in here."

He didn't enter by the double front doors, though, with the coal-oil torch burning above them. He went down the side of the building and sidled in an entrance there. Red waited. Inside, the orchestra struck up and there was a woman's rattling laughter. A minute or so – seeming like a long time – crept by. Then there was a screech, the staccato report of a gun. The music broke off as if a heavy curtain had been dropped over it.

Chess appeared, backing through the open double doors of the front doorway. Crouched, he had both guns out, had them swivelling to cover the interior. He barked something at the throng. Then he was leaping off the steps and flinging himself headlong for the shadows where the ponies waited. There was a wet red stain on the forearm of his left sleeve. Red stood petrified for a few moments, not knowing what to do.

A man appeared in the doorway, his gun drawn. Red's gun hammer cocked, then his finger froze on the trigger. The man in the doorway, staring out into the dark, wore a lawman's badge that glittered on his vest in the light of the coal-oil torch. Red Paine never shot that time.

36

Ed Chess called something to him, already swinging up. Red hit the saddle leather, and they went bolting up the side street for the low hill at that side of the town.

"A holdup!" bellowed some brass-lunged gent in the rear. Then wild blind shots were spurting the road dust in their wake.

Red Paine didn't think too much about it then. Folks lost their heads and hollered anything under excitement. Chess grasped the bridle of Red's horse and steered him off the trail into a little draw.

"Something went wrong – bad, back there," he pantingly explained. "They –" Red looked back to follow Chess' glance.

A horseman who'd been coming down the slope had rounded a wooded bend and sat there watching them from behind. And from the cowtown came the drumming hoofbeats of a fast-organized pursuit. There was no more time for parleying then. They threw the gut hooks to their animals. Something told young Red it was going to be a hot manhunt.

It was. A big lustrous moon floated out from behind a peak in the south to reveal them like a spotlight any time they moved into the open. They emerged from the draw that bent away from the town and into trouble. Some of the posse, warned of the route they'd taken, had cut further up the road and then in over the hills, travelling in a straighter line. They had gained ground. Ed Chess' gun blazed twice. They got into a stretch of timber, came out on a climbing trail that wound toward the jagged peaks of the west.

"They got dang fast ponies," Chess cried once, glancing back. "A second pack coming behind the first one."

The moonlight spilled over his body as they raced into an open spot. And then Red saw the greenbacks sticking out from inside his shirt between the open flaps of his vest. It *had* been a holdup after all.

Rifles began to spit at an angle across the trail. A couple of horsemen had hit up onto a low mound behind to the left. Dismounted, from that point of vantage, they were cracking down. Red had his thoughts busy then with wondering when he'd hit. The road curved and went between cutbanks and they were safe again for a spell. Red's mind was in a turmoil. It looked as if he had been branded an outlaw without knowing it.

They climbed a long gentle slope, angled around a small mesa. The timber grew a little heavier. Chess called to the kid to drive his horse as hard as he could, that they were going to try to throw off their pursuers with a trick soon. Another half-mile and the trail dipped. The pursuit was no longer in sight but they were coming. Ahead a bridge loomed; it spanned a tiny ravine with a creek in its bottom.

Chess threw himself from the saddle on the run as they came up to it. "Follow me now, Red. I know this country from the old days. I'll git you out with your hide whole!"

Red had already dropped from his heaving-flanked lathered horse, and Chess was leading the way down the side of the ravine. In the creek water, he turned to the left. Fifty feet along there was a bend where the rock wall jutted. He didn't quite round it, but seemed to vanish from sight by a stand of thicket. He called. Red led his pony in. Just past the elbow, in its side, was an unsuspected cave-like hole in the wall where a pony or a man could stand comfortably hidden from sight.

"I remember this piece of country like the palm of my hand, Red.... They'll figure that we'll head for the base of the peaks. The brush up there is so danged heavy a man could slip saw from a posse for weeks. They –"

"Chess," Red said stiffly, heart pounding and mouth abruptly dry with the charge he was going to have to make. "Chess, you said you just had a personal grudge to settle back at that dancehall. But it was a holdup, wasn't it? I saw the bills in your shirt."

Ed Chess' eyes seemed to light up like coals in the dark. Then he listened a moment to the sounds of the approaching posse. "Sure, I took dinero; tried to take the whole till, too. It *was* a grudge. A few years back, the partners at that joint threw me out when I was lickered up, then stole my dinero from me when I lay in the alley. I had a grudge, kid. Why –"

"It was still a holdup, Chess. It was owlhoot stuff in the eyes of the Law – and for me too."

The gunman scratched his beard-stubbled jaw as he peered at the kid. "Well, if you want to go scraping for scruples – mebbe you could call it that. I still say I had a personal grudge. Look, Red, you're the son of a famous lobo. How'd you expect to live in life – working in a bank?"

They both dropped into silence as the first half of the posse hit the bridge, their hoofs making the truncheons boom hollowly. The pursuers never hesitated, piling on up the trail. Red answered Chess then.

"Why, I expect to work honest. My dad wanted me to –"

Chess snorted his derision. "Git some sense, boy! Work honest? Do you think they'll let you? You're Big Red Paine's son. You got the owlhoot stamp on you. Men hated your dad – because they feared him. And they'll

40

take it out on you, mind you! They will. You might get work for a spell – here and there. But when they find out who you are – when they's a whisper, somebody who recognizes you – you'll go. You'll get the boot! Git some sense."

Red squirmed in the kak. "But you said you could get me fixed up and –"

"Sure. Still can. Tophand pay, too."

Red was wary, suspicious now. "What kind of work?"

Again they remained silent while the second batch of the posse came along. They passed over the bridge and on up the line. Chess answered.

"Good work, Red. You see, sometimes when they's a mite of trouble on a range or mebbe some rustling or feuding, a cow outfit takes on men who can snap a six-gun real fast and fancy. I been moving around doing that for years now. Good pay. You ain't no outlaw. Honest men hire you to – well, to protect their interests. Why, often you're sorta working right along with the Law, or at least doing a job it can't handle right there." He chuckled. "And I got word of a big spread down at Morgan Valley that needs men of that kind now. And the way you can sling a hogleg, Red, why –"

Red spat it out with harsh dryness. "A

41

hired gunman, eh. That's what it is. Well, not for me!"

"Don't be a locoed fool!"

"Nope! My dad wouldn't uh wanted that for me. No owlhoot. No gunman, either. . . ." One of his hands moved with that incredible quickness, so sharp the result was in evidence even before it was expected. "Chess, you're going your way. I'm going mine."

And Ed Chess was looking down at the gleaming barrel of Red Paine's snatched-out Colts. "You mean that." And it was no question.

"I do, Chess."

"If that posse catches you, my hide will be –"

"I'll wait here half an hour after you leave, Chess. . . . And I don't know where you went. . . . So long."

Chess smiled a little bitterly. Then he hit the kid lightly on the arm, wished him good luck, and led out his pony. Chess dragged the horse up out of the ravine and rode back down the trail they had come up. He would loop around somewhere below and slip out of that stretch of country, Red guessed. He began to sweat, despite the slow cold wind, as he waited it out, keeping his word. What he had determined to do was going to take a heap of nerve, more nerve than anything yet had required of him in his short life. Again and again he had to overpower the terrific impulse to try flight.

Finally, when he estimated a half-hour had passed, he too left the ravine. But back on the road, he crossed over the bridge and set out after the posse. He was going to give himself up, swear he hadn't known the play Chess had rigged, and throw himself on the mercy of the Law. After all, he hadn't fired a shot. It was a case of anything to save himself from being branded an outlaw, of keeping the oath pledge at his dad's grave.

CHAPTER FIVE

Far sooner than he'd expected, he came upon two of them. They were coming back down the trail, a little gent in a white calfskin vest and a big man with huge rangy sloping shoulders and carrot-hued hair. They didn't even spot Red at first as he drew up beside a stand of trees to await them.

His mouth was a bitter line. But he had learned another lesson in life: he had to be on guard against former friends and accomplices of his own father. They might mean well.

That Ed Chess had actually thought he was doing him a favor. But those men would never understand how resolved he was *not* to follow the owlhoot trail.

The approaching pair, walking their tired ponies, passed through a stretch of luminous moonlight. The big one wore no sombrero now. There was a rag of bandage tied around his head and dried blood on his cheek. Further up the line, his horse had shied at a shadow and thrown him heavily into a patch of boulders. He had gashed his scalp and wrenched his right shoulder so that it was impossible for him to throw a gun with his right hand. His pony limped slightly too. So he was returning.

Then Red recognized him and a rock seemed to drop inside his heart as he took in the huge beak of red nose. Also the left hand with first two fingers missing as he raised a quirly to his mouth. His dad had pointed out this man to him from cover once in a town. And Red had seen his picture in a couple of old newspapers. He was the famed Jud Tentrus, a two-legged son of the devil himself when he hit the trigger, a tophand gunman who specialized in cleaning out bad towns. Now he wore a lawman's badge on his coat, having been appointed a special marshal to run out the gun scum of the town back down the line. His dad had told Red that this Tentrus deeply hated badmen the way some gents hated snakes.

"Hey, is that you, Howie?" called out the rider with Jud Tentrus, taking Red for some member of the posse who had dropped back.

Gun in scabbard, hands up, the slim Red rode slowly out into the light. "I'm surrendering," he said. "I'm one of the gents you're chasing for that dancehall holdup. . . . Only I didn't know it was going to be that, a holdup, gents. I swear it. . . ."

The one in the vest whipped out a gun. Tentrus tried to dig for one with his injured shoulder in vain. Then he hooked out one awkwardly with the hand with the missing two fingers, raised it like a club, and bolted his pony at the quiescent Red Paine. He lowered the clubbed weapon when the other man came up and got the hogleg from the kid's holster.

"I said I'm surrendering," Red said quietly.

They scoured him with hard eyes. The smaller one said he guessed Red's nerve had run out on him. But Tentrus, looking deep into the kid's eyes, shook his head.

"No it didn't. Not this young un. . . . Where did your pard, Chess, go?" Chess had been recognized when he tried to jump the dancehall.

45

"I don't know. We just – parted. . . . I'm no rat, anyway."

The little man said he was lying about not knowing what was planned at the dancehall. That this was some kind of trick, that Red was trying to snake his way out by playing innocent.

"I came to meet you and give myself up, didn't I?"

"What's your handle, button?" It was Tentrus asking.

"Paine."

"Hmmm. . . . Tell me about it, how you never guessed it was a holdup, like you say."

Red looked into Jud Tentrus' eyes squarely and told him of meeting Chess, a stranger to him, on the trail. How he never knew he was an outlaw. And how Chess had given him the story about settling a score with some snakes. Tentrus asked him what kind of work he'd done last. Red stated frankly he'd worked in a store in Endicott Flats.

"Groot's place," he answered when Tentrus asked the name.

"Henry Groot?" Tentrus said.

"No. John Groot."

"That's right," Tentrus said with a bleak smile, for his trap that failed. "Well, we'll just take you in and see." The other one wanted to put the manacles on Red. "Don't reckon it's

46

necessary," said Tentrus.

They started to ride back. The night was old when they went down the side street where the dancehall stood. A man on the wooden sidewalk recognized the special marshal, Tentrus and set up a shout that they were bringing in a prisoner. A growing throng was trailing them when they drew up in front of the two-storey dobie jailhouse. Some of the leading citizens accompanied them when they went into the lawman's office.

"Make him tell where his pard hit for," one of them began to rant. "Mebbe this is a trick! Mebbe his pard's hurt, and this polecat gave himself up to lead you off his pard's trail."

Tentrus eyed the man scornfully, waved back the others who tried to crowd excitedly in the doorway. The town had had too many shootings in the past few weeks. They were in that state of mind where they thought impulsively in terms of necktie justice, jumped at conclusions.

"Even if he told us which way the other one headed, he wouldn't have no way of knowing where the man might have turned off or cut around. . . . Paine you're sure you didn't know the game at the dancehall?"

Tentrus pursed his hard mouth. Then there was a commotion out front. A horseman was pushing through the mob. Somebody said it was Holtzer the cowman and that he was wounded. In a moment, he came up the jailhouse steps, a burly man with bulging eyes. He clutched a wounded arm as he told his story, snorting and cursing at intervals. He had been coming down a side trail, farther north along the ridge, leading into the main road. And he'd been jumped, by the men who'd pulled the dancehall holdup he'd just heard about, he supposed.

"One of them was tow-headed. I saw that when he got his headpiece knocked off. I tried to make a fight of it, but three of 'em taking me by surprise was too much," he blustered on. He was a big braggart, out to make a celebrity of himself, boasting of his courage. "I tried to fight 'em off. But I got hit an' knocked from the saddle. They took my fresh stallion, an' left one of their petered-out cayuses. So then –"

"Only two men in the dancehall job," said Tentrus.

"Well, mebbe they was just two," admitted Holter. "I saw the tow-headed fella. And then the triggering started. Then –"

A man in the doorway pointed at Red Paine. "He was in the dancehall holdup. Was he one of the men who jumped you on the trail?"

Red almost began to smile, knowing he

hadn't done that. The tow-haired man had been Chess, of course, alone. Holtzer took another step inside, puckered his brows against the lamplight, studied Red. Then, to Red's astonishment, Holtzer nodded. Holtzer meant to make himself an important figure in town for a few days at least.

"Yep, that was one. I remember his blue shirt. And how he seemed like just a yonker for that kind of a game," Holtzer said heavily. "He *was* the other one out there, I swear it, by Gawd!"

The blood began to darken Tentrus' face as he turned back to the kid. "You could uh got lost out there and run into us by accident, swinging around in them foothills. Paine, if you're a-lying –"

"I gave myself up, didn't I?" Red reiterated steadily.

"You say his name was Paine?" cried a man out on the steps. He pushed in, a squat figure in gray with hair thinning in front. "My name's Patten. I'm the brother-in-law of Adam Blair, the deputy up at Twin Forks, I am," he introduced himself. He looked over Red. "And that's Big Red Paine's boy or I'm blind. An' I ain't!" The son of Big Red, the outlaw-killer!"

He told how he knew. He had gone out with the posse under Adam Blair that had gotten Big Red, riding on a tip that had taken them almost a hundred miles. He didn't mention that Blair the deputy had been out of his own bailiwick, thus without authority, when they trapped Big Red. He went on to tell how afterward some of them had watched from up in the timber to be sure his sons and the friend had gotten out of the country as ordered.

"I saw him, this one," Patten said, indicating Red. "He came riding home from school after the shooting of Big Red. He's his youngest son!"

That did it. Tentrus had been willing to believe Red's story till then. But that, backed by the lying Holtzer's evidence was the clincher. "A blasted outlaw's son!" ground out Tentrus. "No outlaw's word is worth the spit on a barroom floor, by grab!"

"He's lying," Red bit off, throwing up a hand to point out Holtzer impulsively, moving with his usual quickness.

"Snakes beget snakes!" roared Tentrus. "Watch your gun!" he told Holtzer, taking it for granted the kid was going to make a grab. And then he hit Red alongside of the jaw with the clubbed Colts he held.

Red reeled back from the glaring Tentrus, who had a wild look in his eyes now. His hatred of lobos amounted almost to a form of insanity when he was roused. Red tried to talk, tried to call Holtzer a liar again. Why he would help shoot up that gent, take his horse, then cut back to give himself up made no sense. But none of them were thinking straight any more.

"Son of a killer, an owlhooter – and he whines he was playing straight, the dirty little skunk!" yelled Tentrus, beside himself with fury at the thought he had been taken in. "Son of a no-good cowardly polecat, a yella trigger slammer!"

Red swung toward him at that, another insult to his father's memory. He started a blow, Tentrus smashed him again with the gun. Red went to his knees and Tentrus ordered the door closed. And then the kid got a beating.

He came off his knees, instinctively ready to fight back like a cornered animal now. But he was almost helpless, dizzy and reeling on legs that had turned to jelly. Losing the weapon on the desk, Tentrus began to club him around with his hand with the missing fingers. Red spat out blood and tried to attack. But in his condition he was no match for the enraged law officer who was one size short of being a giant.

Red bounced back against the desk, slid along it. Tentrus struck him again. Again.

Red got in a feeble blow; but another thudding punch sent him caroming off a wall into a corner, draping himself over a chair. Tentrus jerked him off it. He was motivated by a righteous wrath, righteous in his own eyes anyway.

"Confess, you lying whelp of a murderer!" he ordered. "Confess what you did – and how you lied! Confess –!"

The final word hit Red simultaneously with another punch that made his head boom. Once again he got off his feet. He could see out of but one eye now. And a blow to the belly smashed the wind out of his lungs. It went on for endless minutes. Tentrus told him he'd beat him into the floor till he confessed.

"I didn't do anything," Red mouthed defiantly. "And my dad was no coward, you liar! My dad –" And his skull was pounded back against the thick-planked door by another blow.

He half spun, plunging forward. But his hand caught the edge of the desk as he went down. Gamely he tried to drag himself up erect, got to his knees.

The door was pushed open and a young girl, flaming-eyed and outraged, stood in it. Red would remember her face for a long time even though he saw it only through a swirling crimson mist. She was slim and very square shouldered for a girl. She had on a blue gingham dress and she was wiping her hands on a towel as though she had just come from work. Her coppery hair hung in trim pigtails down her back. She had a slim oval-shaped face. And the blue eyes in it were as chill as water under frozen ice, yet slow-seething with her rage.

"Oh, aren't you a fine brave bunch of men!" she cried scornfully. "You heroes, beating a helpless kid crazy!"

The delighted cries of the throng outside had died. Her contempt lashed out in the sudden stillness. One man inside said:

"Peg! Git outa here! This is no place for a girl!"

She thrust her legs wide, slapping her hands up akimbo. "No, no. A woman doesn't belong here! This is men's work! This –"

"He's a holdup man, the son of an outlaw, Peg!"

"Did he kill anybody – even shoot them?" she said, her nostrils flaring. "No! But you'll kill him, won't you?" She suddenly grabbed up a quirt laying on a nearby chair, drew it back, threatening Holtzer.

"And you, you lying drunkard! Is anybody taking your word on anything? Did you ever pay for that whisky bill you ran up at the

El Diablo? And you, Tentrus, the great gunfighter! Ha-ha! Why you haven't even got him tied up. Aren't you taking a chance, a dangerous chance?"

There was a pause, silence. Nobody could answer her.

"Well," she finally said, "what's stopping you? Go ahead. Give him the choice of being beat to death – or confessing he did anything you want him to say! Go ahead. . . ."

Tentrus worked his mouth, looking a little chagrined as he recovered his temper. Then he spoke to one of the deputies.

"Take him upstairs to a cell! Mebbe – well, mebbe when we bring in his partner we'll git the whole story. . . ."

CHAPTER SIX

Recovering consciousness the next morning with the sun beating in on his sweat-stinking cot blankets was like entering a world of fresh half-remembered torture. His skull felt swollen to the size of a ten-gallon hat. Nausea had him retching over the side of the cot at the first attempt to move. His blow-bloated jaws seemed to crack at the slightest motion.

And there was the memory of what had been done to him.

He fell back on the blanket. A rat blinked at him with beady eyes from a dim corner. He envied the rat and its vigor as it bounded away. After some time he discovered the bucket of water somebody had put over beside the stool. The sun shimmered off its surface. Somehow he managed to drag himself to it on his hands and knees. He lapped up some painfully. With feeble motions he scooped up handfuls and worked them gently over his bruised, battered face and head. He sat down next to the pail. Downstairs somebody dropped a metallic instrument and the *crang* of it rode in wave after wave through his brain.

Slowly, eyes blinking with the pain of recollection, he rehearsed the events of last night. When he thought of Tentrus, his hands fisted so fiercely it made his arms tremble. Then he came to the key, the crux of it all.

"Blair – again," he muttered. It was Adam Blair the deputy who'd brought about the slaying of his dad for something Big Red had never done. And last night, Tentrus had been about convinced he was telling the truth, even despite Holtzer's story. Then Blair, indirectly, through his cousin, had to take a hand in the fate of a Paine again. "Blair," he said slowly, turning over the

55

word in his sore stiff mouth like something he never meant to forget the taste of. For he had a premonition, though it seemed locoed, that Adam Blair had not played his last part in the role of a Paine.

For a moment, dragging himself back to the cot, he wondered if Charlie, his oldest brother, might not have had the right idea, to get revenge, to get Adam Blair. He sank back on the blanket and semi-consciousness flooded slowly over him, deadening some of the pain. He thought once of that nervy girl, Peg.

It was the scrape of the key in the cell lock, exaggerated fiercely on his raw nerve senses, that brought him around again. It was the jailer with the local sawbones who had been sent around. The gray-whiskered man washed out the head cuts, put some salve on them, bandaged him up; fixed up his battered face, too, with something he guaranteed to bring down the swelling. Then he gave Red something bitter and acrid to swallow, saying it would fix up the inside of his head and lessen the pain.

"Old Injun prescription," he grunted. "Here!" He'd produced a pint of redeye, put some in a tin cup.

When he gulped it, Red Paine thought the lining of his throat would be seared out. But after a few moments he got a comfortable warm feeling in his stomach, and an easement came to his tortured nerves. It was the first time Red had ever tasted whisky. His father was very strict about that. One time, in camp, Big Red had larruped one of the bunch unconscious for seeking to slip some to Charlie.

The pill roller left the rest of the pint there and told him to take a sip occasionally. "You're young. You'll be all right in another day," he predicted as he clamped his way out. "You're as tough as rawhide or you wouldn't be able to lift a dang finger today."

After a while, Red was able to sit up as the day wore away, though any quick movement started the war drums thumping inside his skull. And at intervals his eyelids were grated downward in the swollen sockets as if weighted with chunks of lead. In the afternoon he was able painfully to swallow some of the grub on a tray that had been shoved in a couple of hours before. It seemed to keep all the bitterness and physical pain at arm's length, at least.

Again he thought of that dark copper-haired girl, Peg. Regardless of what happened to him, he didn't suppose he'd ever meet her again. It began to dawn upon him, beyond any argument now, that as an outlaw's son

57

he'd be marked for life, a pariah as far as many people were concerned. He recalled what Harry Westfall used to say about wearing a necktie to school. How he had to be different.

"Maybe that Chess was right, anyway," he muttered once through the buzz of business that floated up from the main line. "Maybe they won't let me be honest. Let something happen – and I got a cocked gun against my head 'cause my dad was forced onto the owlhoot. And they won't let me come off it." He rose, paced slowly across the cell. "No, I gotta try. If I could once show them. . . ." Then he swore softly, an unusual thing for him. And he built a quirly, one of the few he had ever smoked in his life. That seemed to soothe things inside his head, too.

The bars of the cell window were a black-ribbed pattern against the bloody ball of the sun dipping into the west when Tentrus came up to see him. The big manhunter came inside, but left his gun with a deputy outside the cell door first. His right arm and shoulder were in a sling. He was very cold-faced now, with no hint of temper. He asked:

"You got any change to make in your story yet, Paine?"

Red Paine's teeth bared. "Hadn't you better truss me up before you gun-whip me this time?" he taunted, repeating what the girl had

58

flung at them last night.

Tentrus ignored it. "Mebbe you feel like telling us where your pard was headed.... Things'd go easier with you."

Red knew then they hadn't given Ed Chess a catching. He shrugged. Tentrus studied him. As he left he said he'd send up more whisky or tobacco if the kid needed it.

"I don't want anything from you, Tentrus."

As the big man went heavily down the stairs, Red stood inside the cell, shaking from his boots up, shaking with rage. He knew that some day, if he had to come back from Boot Hill's own back yard, he and Tentrus would have to have a showdown. Nobody could take what the famed manhunter had done to him and retain his sense of manhood if he let it go unavenged. Some day....

Another night passed. The next day he felt a heap stronger though still bruised. The old jailer with a pocked, sinful-smiling face told him the temper of the town was changing. Folks were cooling off. And Holtzer, who'd been knocking around the bars getting free drinks because of his notoriety, had gotten mixed up on his story a few times, building it to five men who had jumped him and describing Red Paine as red-haired.

On the fourth day he was released.

Tentrus was waiting in the front office. He

handed Red his gun and gunbelt with the gun chambers emptied. "We're giving you a break, Paine, because you're so young. Mebbe you didn't know what was going on. Mebbe. . . . But steer clear of this town in the future! Two of the deputies will ride down the road a way with you to make sure you get out. Good luck to you," he said.

For a moment, Red had a wild boyish desire to spit in his teeth. He wanted to curse the ground the man stood on. But he did it in the way his dad would have wanted it done, the way he imagined Big Red himself might have done it. He said slowly, quietly:

"Tentrus, a real man doesn't swallow dirt easily. . . . Some day, I pray to Gawd, we'll meet again. That day, you'll find out how much of a man I am. What's left of you will belong to the buzzards. Good day."

The pack animal of Chess' was outside. They mounted and rode down the main drag to where it bent to run into the southwest trail out of the town. A mile down it, atop a low dune in the sage, they left him. He'd ridden on twenty-thirty yards when one of the deputies overtook him at the gallop. He shoved a small wad of bills into Red's hand.

"What the devil's this?"

60

"There's twenty-five bucks there, fella. It's a gift to you from somebody. No, not me. But you'll need it and –"

"Did Tentrus try to buy off his consicence with this?" Red demanded sneeringly.

But the deputy shook his head vehemently. "Gosh, no. It was passed to me on the quiet. But I ain't sure from who. So," he shrugged, "I couldn't give it back if I wanted. The message was it was for good luck." He turned back.

Red worked it into his pocket slowly and went on, well aware he'd need it badly enough. Later, he picked up some grub from a hoeman and stowed it in his saddle roll – java and some dried beans and jerked beef. The next day he went through a pass between those peaks in the west and dropped down into a broad valley. He tried not to think; all his thoughts were tinged with the essence of bitterness.

It was down to the south, two days later, in the big valley, that he picked up a bunkhouse job with a small cow outfit run by a man named Clennihan. He started to build himself into a cowhand, able to ride like part of the animal and to act as a good roper. Harry Westfall had taught him that last, too. He was a quiet one, saying little, working hard. And it was while he was there that he heard of his brother, Charlie, the oldest one.

A couple of cowhands, riding the grubline, stopped off to pass the night. They told what news they knew, mentioned the range war there had been up outside Excelsior. Two big spreads had been feuding it out. There had been a showdown battle at a waterhole before some special state officers came into Excelsior and broke it up.

"She was a real scrap at that waterhole," one of the trail-riding hands said. He'd heard about it from a man who'd been there. "It didn't last so long, he told me. Both outfits had their hired trigger slammers on hand, and four were killed. Four! One man from the Big Umbrella brand. And *he* was the one who got the three on the other side, the Box-Double-D. They said he was some gunfighter. A fella called Charlie Paine, he was. . . . Did you hear about the gambler running off with banker's wife over at Frog Junction?"

Red sat still for a few minutes, then walked out into the night. His brother, Charlie, of course. His role was pretty plain, beyond any real doubt. Charlie, who'd planned to get big dinero quick, had hired out his hardware, had been a hired gunfighter, practically a lobo. Their dad never would have wanted that, Red knew. Walking further over, he perched his elbows on the corral bars and stared up at the inscrutable stars.

He felt grief at Charlie's death, felt older. But he had never really been close to the oldest brother. It was also too bad he was dead. But in a way, Charlie had betrayed their dad. He'd let him down, at least. Red thought of the vow he himself had made at the lonely grave behind the burnt-out house, and solemnly took it again. He had to make good, to stay straight, for his dad.

It was a couple of weeks later, just after dawn one morning. He was lifting down a saddle from a peg outside the bunkhouse to go out and inspect fence. Two days before he had been into the nearby town for supplies. Last night, late, Clennihan himself had returned from town. Now he came down from the main house, knuckling sleep from his eyes, a stout easygoing man but looking grave now.

"I gotta ask you a question, Red. And I want the answer straight, with the bark off." He toed the dirt embarrassedly.

Red smelled what was coming. Clennihan asked him if he were the son of Big Red Paine the outlaw.

"I am – and danged proud of it, Clennihan."

Clennihan sighed. "Well, thanks for the truth, anyway, Red. Git some breakfast, then come in for your time. . . . Danged sorry, Red."

The kid tried to fight back. "Have you ever heard anything against me, boss? Ever seen me do anything suspicious?" he asked stiffly.

Clennihan half turned away, anxious to close the matter. "You was picked out in town the other day, Red. A man said you was smaller but looked a heap like Big Red. An' that you moved exactly like him too."

"So you're telling me to hit the owlhoot or starve, eh?"

"Heck, Red. It ain't me. It's the other ranchers around. We had some trouble on this range a coupla years back, and we all swore to hire no gunhands nor suspicious characters. If I kept you on – well, some of those others are big potatoes. They swing weight at the bank – and I got notes out at the bank. . . . And you, being an outlaw's son – well, they said it was – was being a suspicious character. So. . . ." He moved off with relief as his wife called from the house. Red hung the saddle back up slowly. . . . He muttered:

"I wonder if they're letting Hugo live straight?"

CHAPTER SEVEN

When he pushed on, after crossing Broken Snake River, he looped back eastward. Somewhere he had to find a place where his family name was not known. Somewhere he had to get a job so he could build up a reputation and point to it when aspersions were thrown at him. He had figured that out slowly. He had to build his own background that would be the answer to any charges. The world didn't like the background he had.

But work was scarce. Beef prices had slumped, and with winter approaching too it made the task tougher. The dinero in his pocket was getting low when, over on Starvation Creek, he was offered a job with a spread. The foreman admitted they were expecting some trouble over water rights.

"And I saw you practicing your draw by the creek crossing a coupla hours ago. You handled that shooter like she was one of your fingers, fella," the foreman said. "So if you got plenty of nerve you –"

Red flushed, not suspecting he was being watched back there at the time. He had a trick of doing that often, sometimes doing some target practice as well. He found he had an almost uncanny knack of hitting what he swung his gun muzzle on. And he never tired of swinging the gun on a draw. Harry Westfall used to say that if you didn't shake your hogleg clear of holster leather first, you were as good as licked. And his dad used to nod a vehement agreement.

"You won't have no chores," the segundo urged him. "And it's top pay. We'll give you –"

But Red shook his head. He'd been tempted. This wasn't the kind of business he wanted, though. During the next several days, he called himself a danged fool repeatedly. Still, he knew he wouldn't take another such offer if he got it.

A few days later, about sundown, he followed a stage trail out of a ravine. A signpost by the edge of the trail there read, "Red Hat – Sixteen Miles." Across from the post stood a good-sized general merchandise store with a fresh coat of paint. Fingering the scant dinero in his pocket, he entered the place to see what grub he could pick up. The proprietor was a fat little man with a big grin under thick-lensed spectacles. He came down behind the counter, moving along painfully with the aid of a cane.

"What can I do for you, pilgrim?" he asked cheerily.

Red ordered some dried beans and some java, hesitated, wanting to find out the cost of that much. Bates, the proprietor, started to gossip.

"I'm wondering what in shucks is this country coming to anyway? Had a fella coming in here this last five-six weeks. He's camped out in an old cabin up that next draw. Been giving him supplies on credit. He told me he had money coming to him from a relative. He don't do no work. And today he was in again – for more credit." Lefty Bates made a wry face, but grinned again, pushing over a sack of Durham for Red to help himself.

"So I offered him a job. Me, I ain't so spry any more," the garrulous Bates went on. "And the rheumatics in my back," he touched the spot, "it's been right bad of late. 'Sides, it gits danged lonesome here too. I offered him good pay. And what do you think? He said no. Just too plumb shiftless to work, that big pelican. Now what'll it be next, pilgrim?"

"One question. Is that job still open?"

It was, and Red took it. He gave his name as Raine. . . .

67

The winter came. Everything went all right. The snows were light down that way. In the early spring, business got brisk again. Old Lefty was an easy man to work for and an excellent cook in the bargain. Red had a good room in the living quarters off to one side of the store. His old clothes got tauter as he grew some. He came to know a sense of security that had never been his before. He wanted more than this, but this was a start toward something.

One evening, impulsively, he told Lefty Bates he'd given him a fictitious name. The proprietor shrugged.

"A man's name, what is it?" he said philosophically. "If he's a polecat and changes his handle from Brown to Hassard, he's still a polecat, ain't he? An hombre's name is only what he makes it. And I saw right off you had an honest eye. Your move, Red," he said, thumbing down at the checkerboard between them.

For some reason he didn't quite understand himself, Red kept up his shooting practice. The handling of a gun fascinated him. Old Bates used to watch him at it, finally insisted on contributing the shells from the store's supply. He'd crow with delight when Red would place an empty shell on the back of his outstretched hand, and then go for his holster and put a slug into a tin can on a stump before the shell had bounced to the ground.

"You're right pretty with that hogleg, Red. Right pretty. Slicker'n slobbers. That gun, she seems like a part of your hand, all right, all right. None of them crack gun slicks I've heard about – and I seen a few when I was young – ever was any slicker!"

At intervals he'd hitch up his buckboard and go into town to see about ordered supplies coming through. He always came back primed with latest news. Jason Guard who ran the hay and feed store in Red Hat had gotten orey-eyed once too often, fallen asleep with his pipe still going, had his place burnt out. Everson who ran the hotel was going to sell out and go back East. The sheriff had wounded and captured a gunman, Bibault, when he had been tipped off the Panhandle killer was hiding in a cabin out on the sage flats beyond the town.

"Bibault was an old-timer, Red. They say once he held up and robbed four banks in one week. He used to be a devil with the womenfolk too. Being an outlaw on the owlhoot must be a wild life, eh, Red?"

It was plain he was impressed by the romantic side of the outlaw life. Red could have given him some different facts on it. But he only grinned.

On his return from his next trip into Red Hat, Bates brought along a wanted man handbill for three lobos who'd held up a stage over in a corner of the state. The main one was Ira Creeling, wanted dead or alive, with a reward of five hundred on his head. The picture of him on the poster, which Bates was tacking up on a post across from the store counter, showed him to be an ugly-faced cus with a scar over one temple and a thick black mustache. The description said he was heavy-set but only five-feet-two in height.

"They made their getaway after the stage hold-up," Bates chattered away, as if giving the background of some prize item in a collection. "But a posse over there shot two of their ponies from under 'em. They're in real trouble. And Sheriff Lott told me they's been reports they're over this way in the last week." He tapped the picture of the ugly Creeling. "Little. But he must be a big hunk of poison. He was run outa Bridger City, and a jasper's got to be plumb bad to be run outa that rip-roarin' town. Yes-sir-ee. When you're thrown outa a snake-hole, you really must be a hellion. . . . How about some supper, Red?"

That was on a Friday evening. Tuesday

came around. It rained all day, a slow bone-chilling drizzle. In the afternoon, Red was out in the shed in the backyard doing some chores. He entered his room in the living quarters, heard the jangle of the bell hung over the store announcing the arrival of a customer. He moved toward the doorway that connected with the store, automatically noting by the sound of boot heels that there were three of them. Then he heard old Lefty Bates greeting them.

"Howdy, gents, what's your pleasure? One right wet day, ain't –" Then his voice jumped to a surprised pitch. "Why, you're –" He started like a man recognizing a famous character. He broke off, choking as if he'd like to swallow words.

A sharp dry voice barked, "All right. So you know me! Stand back clear of that counter, ya old fool!"

Red stepped quickly through the doorway into the store, then realized that he'd made an impulsive mistake. The doorway came in on the side opposite the counter. He was in the open, fully exposed. The man at the counter with the gun out on Bates half wheeled toward Red. The pair with him went for their hardware. Red stood there in an old rain-dappled black coat that hid the gunbelt slung underneath. He had figured on doing a

71

little shooting practice out back.

The one at the counter was Ira Creeling, the wanted man, Red saw at once. There was the forehead scar. He had shaved off the mustache in an attempt at self-disguise. But the white line where it had recently been showed. And he was no taller than a young boy. He was the hombre too tough for even Bridger City to stomach. One of his companions moved swiftly down on Red, the man's gun muzzle aimed at the middle of his chest. Red half-lifted his hands to shoulder level.

"We came in for some grub," Creeling said. "But now, boys, we'll take the grub — and take these two along with it. They'll make nice hostages!"

Red knew what that would mean eventually. Death. He seemed slouched, resigned, as the gunman walked up and put out a hand to run over him for weapons. Then he worked that trick Ed Chess had pulled on him in the alley back at Endicott Flats. He snapped his left hand down, bringing the lower side of it like a blade chopping on the gunman's wrist. The gun crashed into action. But the bullet of the deflected weapon went harmlessly down past Red's right side. In a split second, he had seized the man by the edges of his slicker front, jerked him forward hard. Simultaneously, Red lowered his head. The gunman's face cracked viciously on the top of the kid's skull. Blood spurted from the jasper's face and he reeled, half conscious, on his feet, helpless.

The other pair couldn't pull the trigger with the third one acting as a shield for Red Paine. Then Red had plucked his own ivory-butted Colts free as fast as a cow's tail in fly time; he had it spurting lead as he let the sagging man flop free. It all happened in the space of a deep-drawn breath. Creeling, crouched in a squat like a frog, started to ride that trigger. The yammer of the guns exploded against the four walls and the ceiling. Ira Creeling missed for the last time in his life. With an icy calm that was confidence incarnate, Red Paine took aim. He shot like a man born to the gun. His first slug took Creeling in the knee, pitched him against the counter so he was too off balance to aim well. His second bullet wiped out that scar on the badman's forehead as it ploughed its way into his brain, snuffing out his life immediately.

The third one was already at the front door. He got a shot through the hat; and went diving off the porch. When Red got out there, the man was already hightailing it up the trail on one of the ponies. The rain had abruptly begun to torrent down, the water thick as a screen. Any kind of shooting was useless as the fleeing rider was screened from sight in a few more yards. When the outlaw's son reentered the store, old Bates was standing over the one dropped by Red's head butt, brandishing an axe handle.

"Yippee, son! You sure are a shootin' fool!" he crowed. "Outgunned Creeling himself! Yow! And captured another when you was drawing against three snakes who had you covered! I never heard of anything like it! Never, no siree!"

Red stood solemn-eyed, mouth clamped tight against the way his insides were pitching, the scene clouding and swaying before his eyes. Creeling lay there as if slumbering against the base of the store counter, his head half cushioned on the red puddle formed beneath it. Red Paine had killed his first man. For a moment, even though the man was a killer, he wished he could bring him back to life. Killing was so terribly decisively final. He knew then deep in his heart that though he might be compelled to use a gun many times more before he died, he would never slay except as a final desperate resort.

"Ol' Creeling will never slay another man, by grab!"

Bates' last remark pulled Red out of it. He kept the second man covered while the storekeeper got some rawhide thongs. They trussed him up, carried the corpse into the storeroom in back, Lefty still chortling over what a job Red had done. They decided that first thing in the morning they would take the two into Red Hat in the wagon. Red himself was entitled to the five hundred reward on Creeling.

But they never had to hitch up the wagon for that job. A couple of hours later, as they sat down to supper, Sheriff Sam Lott and a five-man posse pulled up at the store. Bedraggled and disgruntled, they tramped into the store, Lott cursing the heavy rain. They said they'd been close on the coat-tails of Creeling when the downpour had wiped out all trail signs.

"We got him for you!" Lefty Bates announced triumphantly.

The lanky balding Lott, who looked more like a Bible-pounding preacher than a badge packer, wouldn't believe it till he saw Creeling and the captured gunman with his own eyes. Lefty Bates related the yarn glowingly, describing exactly how Red "Raine" had done it single-handed even though covered by the gun slicks. The tall Lott blew out his breath, forgot the tin cup of redeye in his hand and stared hard at Red.

"You had the nerve to make a play when it

was three to one and your smokewagon was still holstered? Then you outshot Creeling himself?"

Red shrugged. "Reckon they didn't expect it." He had been conning that over in his mind. Using speed and the unexpected, a man could get away with a big gamble. He figured it was a new lesson he had learned.

Samuel Lott pushed out his hand. "I could use a deputy like you, Raine. I *sure* could. . . ."

CHAPTER EIGHT

When he'd been a deputy in Red Hat scarcely a week, the outlaw's son walked in single-handed on a gun slick who'd barricaded himself in a cabin on the low bluff over the town. The jasper, passing through, had gone berserk on a bellyful of redeye, shot up a barroom, wounded two men, and holed up in the cabin when cut off from his pony. He had the old man who owned the place in there with him and threatened to blast his brains out if they rushed the place. Nobody knew what the devil to do.

Without a word, under the high-noon sun,

Red Paine holstered his ivory-stocked .45 plus the mated gun he'd bought, put a match to his quirly, and walked toward the cabin. The man inside bellowed a warning. Red told him he was coming in without shooting. The man sent a slug screaming out the window just over his head, threatened to put the next one through his hostage.

"Kill him and I'll come in there and club your brains out," Red said flatly, never varying his measured stride. "If you want to live, let me in. I'll guarantee you won't be shot." He kept on coming.

He figured in that heat the liquor would be dying inside the wild gent, and he figured on the unexpectedness of it. The man sent another bullet that jetted dirt beside his left boot. He started to bawl another threat, but his voice fell before he finished it. Red walked up to the cabin door and kicked it in.

"Show some sense now and come out," he said. If he had tried to jump a gun then, he would have been dead in a wink, shot from the dim interior. An agonizing thirty seconds dragged by. The watching witnesses, well back, held their breaths. Then the man threw his still smoking weapons through the doorway and shambled out after them. The outlaw's son put the handcuffs on him. Somebody cheered.

The man known as Red Raine was established in the town.

As the weeks went by, he made few friends, always holding himself on guard, staying to himself. The fewer folks he knew, he figured, the less happenstance there was that his true identity might become known. This was his big chance, he believed. Once he built up a reputation as a four-square straight John Law, the way he had it planned, he could shed the mask, tell him he was Big Red Paine's son, and there would be no stigma attached to him. The one thing he hated was going under false colors. He was proud of his own name.

Everything went along fine. Lott liked him because he didn't drink. His other deputy, Dultro, had a liking for the bottle, though he could always attend to the job. One sultry afternoon, Red rode into town with a horse thief he'd brought back from a pueblo down the line where a justice of the peace had grabbed him. The town buzzed with excitement. The southbound stage had passed through a short while before. Aboard it, they told him, had been Adam Blair, the famous manhunter, risen to a full sheriff now. He had even stopped in at the hotel bar for a drink, shaken hands with Lott and

78

the other deputy.

Red Paine's mouth jerked tight and the blood roared in his head at mention of the name of the man who'd burnt down his father on a false charge. He knew he might have challenged Blair to a duel if he'd come face to face with him. He got himself cooled off. Then a second creeping fear possessed him. Perhaps Blair, hearing about the young deputy who was gaining some fame himself, might have noticed the similarity between Red Raine and Red Paine. Might have asked for a description of him, then passed on his information to Red's boss.

But when the dour straight-laced Lott returned to the office after dinner at his white cottage up on the hill, he gave no sign of anything wrong. He even offered Red a cigar, then grinned when he caught the growl of thunder up in the northwest.

"Reckon we'll have a storm . . . My paw, he was a lawman too. He always said as how rainy nights were good for the John Laws. Men stayed home and stayed outa trouble."

It was in August that they went into the hills after the small bunch of two-bit rustlers who'd been running the Bar-T stuff up on the creek near Bates' store. They cut their sign, killed one in a running fight, and cut another off from the bunch, capturing him. His name was Powell. When they put him in jail, Red noted his expensive rig, the new boots with the chased silver spurs, his silk shirt, the guns with the pearl-handled stocks. Powell was exceptionally well turned out for a small-time rustler, a tall knife-faced man with a cast in one eye.

Two days later a gent sent word in from the hills he had a tip on where the rest of the bunch were. His message said he would speak only to Red Paine because he trusted him. Lott allowed as how it was probably just some crank who'd seen a couple of riders in the night, but sent Red out. Red got to the little combined barroom and eating place out on the stage road where the writer said he'd be waiting. He went in warily, hand stemmed on a protruding gun butt and asked for "Big John" the name signed on the scrawled note. The bar boss looked stupid.

"He's going to be late gitting here," called out one of a pair sitting at a table back in a rear corner. There was a window beside the table but it was shuttered.

Red walked down there. It was hard to tell much about their faces in that light and with their hats jerked down low. But he could see they too were expensively garbed. The bigger one wore a large diamond ring on each hand. He said softly:

"Deputy, we don't want no trigger-pulling, so don't go off half cocked. They's a gent outside that window covering you through the crack. And me, I got my hand on a gun under this hat." He nodded at the brand-new pearl-gray sombrero on the table before him. "But we don't want trouble."

Red Paine's gray eyes enlarged, got a stony shine behind the smoke from the Durham tube in his mouth. "And I got my hand on this gun in my belt. I shoot fast too – very very fast. Start trouble – and somebody gets hurt – bad. Where's this Big John?"

The one with rings smiled. "He's going to be awful late getting here, Deputy – because there ain't no Big John."

"Maybe you'll change your mind and find him when I drag your pants down to jail," Red came back casually as if making a remark about the weather.

"Mebbe you won't drag 'em down, Deputy Red *Paine*. . . ."

It hung there on the fetid air of the barroom for seconds, Red's real name. The big man said sit down and have a drink and a friendly little parley. Red, with the sweat like ice particles inching down his spine, said maybe he had made a mistake about who he was talking to. Red said he was Deputy Raine. The man chuckled as if he had gravel in his throat.

He said gently, "Remember the night Jud Tentrus brought you in? . . . Yeah. I was in the pueblo that night. I recognized you in Red Hat yesterday. Now be good, will you? And listen."

Red tongued out his quirly butt and heeled it, nodded.

The man blew on one of his diamond rings. "Down in your mangy jailhouse, you got a man named Powell. We want him out of there."

Red said nothing merely shrugging.

"A little help from you and I reckon we could get him out, eh? Be easy, wouldn't it? And there'd be no hard feelings and a secret would still be a secret, wouldn't it? Why, you'd still be deputy." He chuckled again.

Red had it then as he took in again the fine clothes of the seated pair, thought of the rig Powell wore. Powell hadn't been a regular member of those mangy rustlers. Just riding along with them, evidently, when the Law had hopped in. Powell was probably a big potato among the owlhoot gentry somewhere. And it was important to get him out.

"I am deputy," Red answered finally. "And

I'll stay a straight one – or quit. So, mister, go to blazes."

"I thought Big Red's son would be a smart un."

"And honest!" He blew at a hovering deerfly. "When you give the sign to the gent outside to start slamming, I'm putting lead right down your throat."

The big man went a little greenish, dropped his eyes to Red's hand on the ivory gun butt. "We don't want no shooting," he reaffirmed quickly again. "There'd be a pretty little piece of dinero in this for you, too. Mebbe five hundred. Yes?"

Red spat on the floor. "If you'd said five thousand I'd still spit. Now do you see how the wind blows?"

"Too bad Sheriff Lott is going to have to be slipped the word who you are."

"Sure is . . . but Powell'll still be scratching the bedbugs in that jailhouse after I'm gone."

The big man blew on a ring again. "We could make that offer six hundred, mebbe."

"When does the snake outside the window get to blasting? My trigger finger needs exercise," Red impatiently said. He backed, keeping his face toward them, veered over to the bar. He called the drink wrangler out in front of the counter. Then taking him along as a shield, Red moved to the door, cutting an eye at it repeatedly lest he be taken from the rear there.

But there was no shooting. He mounted his pony and rode back toward Red Hat unmolested. But he was cursing spasmodically in the dry hard voice. Always, ever and again, his past, something out of it, bobbed up to endanger his present.

When he returned to the town, he decided to go to Lott, give him the story, and admit he was Big Red the outlaw's son. But Lott was away that night. When the morning came, Red had decided to stand pat and wait to see what did happen. Nothing did for two days. Powell sat up in his cell and played endless games of solitaire with a certain smug air that hinted he knew things would be all right soon. No strangers like the pair Red had talked to were seen around town. Lott came in from a trip out on the range that afternoon and told Red he wanted him to sleep in the jailhouse that night. It was Red's night off, but Dultro had been hitting the bottle heavily, the sheriff said.

Before he bedded down on the office cot, Red checked on Powell in his cell. The man was asleep. Red pulled off his own boots and stretched out a little after midnight. It was just short of four o'clock when there was a knock on the door and Lott's voice called from outside. Red could see that as he scratched a match and glanced at the old clock on the shelf in the corner. When he let the sheriff in, Lott ignored his greeting and told him to light the lamp.

The yellow glow bloomed like a slow-opening bud from the cracked chimney and Red looked up. Up into Samuel Lott's gun muzzle like a third eye below the two harsh angry ones in his parsonlike face.

"I gave you a chance, Paine," he grated out. "But it seems like it don't pay!"

Red met the gaze steadily. "All right. So somebody's told you I'm Big Red Paine's son. Yes, I am. But I'm straight and –"

Lott banged the desk top with a fist. "Nobody told me. I've known it for a long spell! Right after you first come in. . . . Was going through some old reward handbills I found in a desk drawer. One of 'em had a picture of your father on it. And I saw the resemblance – and why you was so uncanny handy with a shooting iron! I knew then. But I gave you a chance."

Red was too keyed up to catch the thinness of that explanation then. He was surprised Lott had known all along. "I've played it dang straight. You can't prove I've ever –"

"Stop blatting lies," Lott said with the tension of a man struggling to retain his control. "I got word a while ago. They's going to be a jailbreak tonight – with you on duty. Somebody in on it got Dultro drunk a-purpose."

Red just shook his head dazedly, trying to think it out. He had refused to do business with that pair out in the hills. "I – I turned down a bribe," he muttered. Then he stabbed a finger at the sheriff. "Wait – wait and see if anybody does get out of this cuartel tonight. That'll prove –"

Samuel Lott laughed jeeringly. "Naturally, you little buzzard, now that you're warned, you'll play it straight. Think I'm a fool?"

Red's eyes widened, got that stony shine. His gunbelt and Colts hung on that wall peg about a yard away. Still, he would have gambled on his incredible speed to get them and make his play. But that would only confirm Lott in his suspicions. He wanted so badly to clear himself, to convince this law boss that he was a fit and honest representative of the Law.

Lott went on heavily, "Yes, I trusted you. And what? I got this word. A gent slips up to my house to warn me. After he left, I yanked on my boots and followed him to find out more. He said you were in on it. I didn't want to believe him. I found him in that little gully behind my place. I stumbled over him, Paine. Stumbled – over – him. He was dead, knifed in the back! The man who came and warned me – and warned me against *you* down here. . . ."

Red couldn't savvy it. He knew it wasn't so, yet found himself half believing it like something you see in a very real dream. "I don't know a blamed thing about it, Lott."

"Somebody's got to explain that dead man come morning," Lott said, thudding the desk again. "There was a friend in the house when that fella came. My friend heard what was said. Tomorrow this whole town's a-going to be talking. What're you going to say? Tell 'em to forget a corpse who got killed – because he told a story involving you among others?"

Red Paine moved away from those tempting Colts on the wall. He lifted his hands in surrender. "All right, Lott. Take me prisoner!"

Lott gulped so that the gun jumped in his hand. He seemed taken aback for a moment. Then some of the sternness left his face. He worked his mouth as if coming to a decision. "Paine, I never had no boy of my own. . . . Mebbe you made a little mistake, mebbe you didn't." He sighed. "But come morning, this town won't listen to reason. That dead gent in the gully, he's got relatives here. . . . Me, I

87

dang near believe you're innocent."

Red said nothing. He was getting hardened to this, steeled to what happened to an hombre because he hadn't picked another kind of a dad.

The sheriff pushed back his hat. "Red, I could be busted outa office for dereliction of duty. . . . But your hoss is out in the shed. Take him and ride. . . . Slip out quietlike. . . . I'll tell 'em some story."

A little while later, no badge on his shirt now, Red Paine was taking the trail up the bluff to the south of Red Hat. Once again the bitterness of frustration ate like a live thing into his sick heart. But he couldn't blame the Law this time. Lott had helped all he could. . . .

CHAPTER NINE

Even the next day, as he pushed on through rough broken country following a few hours of rest after dawn, he mulled it over in his mind. He had a sort of dead dull feeling, wondered if there was any sense in trying to go straight any more. Maybe Ed Chess was right. But he still would like to know how the thing had been rigged; it teased his curiosity. He had not entered into any conspiracy to sell out the Law and get that Powell snaked out. Yet that gent had come to Lott's place, named him, afterward paid with his life for giving the information.

He could make no sense out of it. Driving him from town wouldn't help get Powell out of jail. Not with Samuel Lott, his hackles up, on guard. The thing was a mystery.

That day, covering his trail as much as possible, cutting from the road to cross a ridge, he avoided two towns and all habitations. Some instinct warned him to leave as little trace as possible. He realized he had all the reactions of a fugitive, and it was maddening because his hands were clean. That night he slept little when he camped in a draw. The thing gnawed in the back of his mind, refused to let him rest completely. He had been neatly double-crossed somehow, been cast in the role of a Judas by somebody. But why? They wouldn't get Powell free that way. Rather, it would make it that much tougher to accomplish.

The next forenoon, he dropped down into a hollow, where there was a tiny settlement, to pick up some supplies. He packed them in his saddle roll after leaving the store, was just swinging into the saddle when he noticed a man inside the open door of a cabin across the road. Instinct sent one of Red's hands sliding down to an ivory gun butt. For the man was just grabbing a shotgun from beside the doorway.

No words were spoken. The man sort of let the shotgun fall back against the wall, grinning nervously. He moved off into the cabin. Red touched the spurs to the roan he now rode. But when he got around the elbow of a low hill, he cut quickly into the trees, rode up to a point of vantage whence he could look back down upon the handful of cabins and the store. The man was out in the road, talking excitedly to a handful of folks around him. Red scowled. It wasn't as if he were wanted for anything. Finally he decided the man must have taken him for Big Red the former outlaw. When he came to a canyon that branched off to the west, he left the south trail, though.

He didn't know what he would do next and cared less. Sometimes he thought of Harry Westfall and wondered what he would say now. Again he remembered how Harry used to say he was different from other boys at school. Harry didn't know how true that was going to be when he matured into the man he now was. It seemed as if the world wouldn't let him be anything but different because of the parents of whom he'd been born; always, he was suspect.

It was just getting dusk when he rounded a curve on the road that ran beside a shallow, muddy-watered stream and came upon the cowtown sprawling out from the base of the wooded ridge on his left. His first impulse was to ford the stream and avoid it and keep going. Then a dull anger boiled in him. After all, he was guilty of nothing. Actually, he was no culprit, no fugitive. Defiantly he turned into it past a cluster of dobie hovels, forked over a hump and into the wide main street. The yellow glow of lamps were just splashing on in the darkness.

His defiance went a step further and a reckless wildness jumped up in him. No more was he a penniless saddle tramp. He carried most of that five hundred reward he'd collected on Ira Creeling plus the savings from his salary as a deputy. He tilted the high-curved brim of his flat-crowned gray hat rakishly. Perhaps it was the reaction to the strain and anxiety. Anyway, he decided to have himself the devil of a time. Some drinks. A real mess of hot grub he didn't cook in a skillet over a lonely camp. And he'd dance too, by grab. He wanted a heap of people around him. He laughed low in his throat as he guided his cayuse around the crowd surrounding a freighter wagon whose rear wheel had come off. Nobody paid him so much attention as a glance.

At a livery barn he left the horse to be grained and groomed. The beardless button there said that *The Golden Gulch* was the best honky tonk in town. Stretching saddle-cramped legs with delight, he found it down past the Cattleman's Bank, a wide building fronted by a long wooden awning. Through a window he could see a good crowd bellied to the long bar beside the dance floor, the rouged girls moving in and out amongst them. Inside, a piano already beat out a fast tune. The warm invitation of the place reached out to him.

Near the rear end of the bar, he found an open space, slapped down his hat so that dust eddied up around it, told the drink wrangler he wanted the best gila juice in the joint and to leave the bottle in front of him. He threw down a twenty-dollar bill. Maybe if he got orey-eyed, the world might look a heap rosier.

Down the bar, a man said, "Want you to meet my brother, honey," as he introduced another gent to a girl with yellow hair and bee-stung lips.

Red lowered the drink he'd picked up, thinking of Hugo. Sadness flooded through him. His dad had had such high ambitions for them all, wanted them to be a real family as well as successful. Now Charlie, the fool, was in some Boot Hill, and Hugo Paine had vanished. Suddenly Red knew what a lone wolf existence he'd had. The one man he'd known as a friend had been old Lefty Bates out at the store. He put a match to his quirly, forgot the former till it scorched his fingertips. He swore and shook it out just as the perfume of a near-by woman reached his nostrils.

"Don't move. Don't look around – or give any sign," her voice came low. The tension in it told him there was danger. "You're being watched right now."

He knew then she was standing directly behind him. He cut his eyes just enough to catch a glimpse of copper-hued hair piled high on her head. Her back was to his. An orey-eyed gent came along and wanted her to dance. She laughed back and said later. The gent moved off. Her voice came again.

"Paine, you're a fool. . . . A fool! Don't you know you're wanted?" Then she was exchanging badinage with another customer, giggling at his clumsy compliments.

Red's hand on the glass jerked so he spilled half the contents over his fingers. She knew his name. That was what hit him. He took a deep drag on the quirly. "Wanted? For what? I reckon you're mistaken, miss. I –"

"Listen. You're wanted for that jailbreak up in Red Hat where Rio Powell got away. Your description was telegraphed down here. Are you insane to walk into a town like this, Paine?"

"Jailbreak in Red Hat? ... There was none. Why –" He was completely mystified now. At the same time he was wondering where he'd heard that voice before. ...

"Sheriff Lott back there seems to think there was one. Powell was discovered missing at sunrise. You were gone too. The telegram blames you for his escape. Or maybe that sheriff is crazy.... The boss is telling the houseman at the front door now. They're looking your way. Give no sign."

It was so insane the shaken Red's next remark made no sense as his panicked mind sought for the key to the thing. "I didn't kill that man in the gully. Lott knows –"

She cut in in a quick whisper. "The report says nobody was killed. It was a clean getaway. That you were bribed. And that you're Big Red the outlaw's son.... Hello, Joe. How're you tonight?" Her voice rose as she greeted another customer.

The palms of Red Paine's hands were slick with sudden sweat. He didn't understand

94

things. But a getaway was the essential thing now. His arms slid off the bar lip ready to smoke a way through if he had to.

Her voice murmured to him. "Don't go for the side door. They got that covered too now, Red." She sounded terribly discouraged. "Wait. . . . The music's about to start. They'll be dancing. Get into the crowd on the floor. They won't dare shoot then. . . . Then take the stairs to the balcony and –" Her voice became just a warm shaky whisper. "Good luck, Red. . . ."

After a few moments, he edged his head around casually after telling the barkeep to give him some cigars. She, whoever she was, was gone.

The piano thumped. The violin scraped. A fat Mexican grinned over the accordion he pumped on the little platform in one corner, and couples began to whirl on the nearby dance floor. Putting on a wide smile, Red swaggered over to it as if to pick himself a partner. He glided amongst several couples, getting a curse when he bumped one pair. Quickly, darting and cutting, he worked down toward the stairs in the rear that led to the gallery. As he took them two steps at a time he saw a house guard at the side door pointing his way.

Above, he found the hall that ran to the rear

of the building. At the end of it was a back stairs. Flinging down them, he went out a rear door and into the night, a hunted man again. He got to the livery barn along a back lane coming into the grazing lot. It seemed to take hours for the boy to get the roan resaddled, an eternity in which he stood away from the lamp, a ready gun held close to his leg. But they evidently were still seeking him back around the dancehall.

He left town, splashed through the wide shallow creek reflecting the fat yellow moon, turned downstream. And Fate had to take a final whack at him. A rider appeared from a cut running down to the bank.

"Hey, stranger," he called. "If you're going down, the road's on the other side. It's much better goin'."

Red just waved and kept riding. But he had been seen.

He pushed on into the night. When a coyote bayed over on a spiny little ridge, he felt a certain kinship. He too was an outcast, hated by men. But now a new force rose in him. In turn, he hated men, mankind. They called him bad because he had happened to be born the son of an hombre forced to ride on the wrong side of the fence. But he had learned that, with few exceptions, regardless of which side of the fence they rode on, men were greedy and tricky, crooked and vicious.

Some hid behind a cloak of respectability, even wore the badge of the Law. They affected to despise his breed, hunted him down even when there was nothing against him. But given the opportunity, especially if they figured to get away with it without being caught, they would do anything any so-called outlaw would do. The big difference was that the lobo had the nerve to admit he was busting the Law and defied it to catch him.

For it had burst on him with a startling, blinding clarity what actually had happened back in Red Hat, and how he had been duped into being the scapegoat, into practically pinning the guilt on himself. The pious-looking Lott, the sheriff, had sold out to those men who'd tried to bribe him, Red himself. Unable to intimidate him, the one with the diamond rings and his pard had obviously gotten in touch with Lott and bought his integrity. It was so plain now Red Paine gnashed his teeth in a fury at having been fooled.

Perhaps Dultro, the other deputy, had been in on it too. No matter. It would have been simple to get him lickered up and off the scene. That gave Lott the excuse to assign him to the jail that night. And of course, Lott had lied about having recognized him as

Big Red's son much earlier, having recognized him from an old handbill bearing a picture of his dad. Red remembered now that until a year or so before his death, his dad had worn a mustache. That would have hidden what likeness there was between them.

No, that pair had tipped off Lott on his identity. And Lott, the danged hypocrite, had used it as a lever to put him in flight. The yarn about the man stabbed in the gulch after bringing him information of a threatening jailbreak was so much whole cloth. Swinging to the motion of the roan, Red threw an angry wordless cry into the night. He wanted to lash out, to hurt somebody, anybody, in return for the way he'd been repeatedly hurt.

After sending him away from Red Hat with the badge of guilt pinned on him, it had been a simple matter for Lott to release Powell, go home, then at dawn spread the alarm, show the jail with the prisoner and Red the deputy gone.

"It was dad-blamed slick," Red bit off aloud. There was no possible doubt. If Lott had been playing it straight, if what he had told were true, forewarned, he could have prevented any escape that night.

And now Red himself was being hunted.

It was much later in the night, when he paused to give the roan a breather in a gulch, that the other came to him. He had been thinking of the woman who'd warned him in the dancehall. How she'd known his name. And there was something about her voice, a certain familiar note faintly discernible in the mists of memory. The fog of time suddenly opened a rift. Through it he saw again that night he'd been with Ed Chess . . . Given himself up . . . Been taken in by Jud Tentrus . . . The beating in the jailhouse . . . And then the appearance of the copper-haired girl in the doorway to flay them with her scornful fury, to halt the beating. Peg had been her name; he'd never forgotten that single scrap of information about her. Peg. . . .

And it had been Peg, as a dancehall girl back there, who had just warned him, saved him again. It was the same voice. . . .

CHAPTER TEN

They were closing in on him. He could tell that the next day. A little after sunup, he'd crawled into a thicket and caught a few hours of restless dream-shot shuteye, then hit the leather again. And he'd seen the shifting dust pall miles back up the valley to east behind him. They were still far behind, but they'd started with fresh ponies. He hadn't. And he was in strange country.

He got into the hills, munching on some cold grub in his saddle roll and looping in an arc northward. Hitting a stream, he turned into it and rode down into a canyon, thus leaving no tracks. He rested the horse in the canyon awhile. But emerging from it, luck broke against him again. He rode smack into three-four cowhands catching a smoke inside a fence-line just back from the creek bank.

"Howdy, pilgrim," one of them hailed him. "Say, did you notice any strays up there in Little Horse?"

"What?" Red asked, pushing his jaded body erect in the hull. Then he realized Little Horse must be the name of the canyon. "I'm in a heap of a hurry, gents." And then he turned the roan into the track that bent off to the south. Even as he did so, he realized it was the worst thing he could have said.

An hour later, the roan dragged him up the far side of a broad basin. The next instant he had slapped off his hat, flung from the kak. He pulled the horse down from the lip, then peered over again himself. Emerging from a draw to the south some distance away in the clear a pack of riders. Not ordinary cowmen, either. The sunlight slanted off the guns in their saddle boots. And even as he watched, he saw the same sun catch the lens of a pair of field glasses with which one of them scoured the open country.

It was a second posse. The alarm had been spread over the country all right, as Peg had warned him in the dancehall.

Back in the basin bottom, he turned westward, reached a jungle of chapparal. Its high black stalks hid a man even in the saddle. He took a winding animal path through it, once came upon a pair of old mosshorns at a crosspath. They went stampeding away, smashing through the growth. It sounded like a terrible thunder in his ears, thunder men must hear for miles. But he made it safely to the ragged ridge in the northwest as the sun went down. Two things gradually seeped into his fatigue-dulled, overstrained mind. One was that this Rio Powell must have been an important prisoner for them to take such pains to get the man supposed to have freed him. The other thing brought back something he'd once heard his dad say. It was that there was one thing a snake wouldn't spit on, namely a lawman who turned bad. And, Red realized, that was what he was branded now.

Soon the whole world took on a nightmarish quality. He was half dead, his belly yelling for grub, his body wracked with fatigue. The roan could barely drag itself on, falling back to a walk again and again so he had to spur-prod it roughly. On the other side of the ridge, he came onto a cart track, followed it, cursing the luminous moon that splashed a clear if ghostly glow over the countryside every time it dodged out from behind the long ribbons of cloud. Off in the distance to the south, a rifle cracked once, then twice quickly after a short pause. He knew it was the signal of a posse. He began to think in terms of the showdown stand he would make.

For to surrender himself would be just about knotting a hempen necktie around his own neck. It would be Sheriff Samuel Lott's word against that of Red, the son of an outlaw.

Moving like a drugged man, he was trudging beside the boogered-down roan when the trees ended suddenly. Ahead there was a big clearing with fields in it. And over to the right a cabin with light showing behind its shaded window on his side. Smoke drifted up from the tin pipe above the roof. As he moved closer he caught the warm taunting aroma of boiling java.

Leaving his pony ground-anchored, he worked in toward that window, edging past the wall, hand clamped hard on the butt of a drawn Colts. The shade was up a couple of inches. He peeked through the crack. Two men sat inside at a table. Their talk came to him through one of the rag-stuffed panes.

"So Tentrus is a U.S. marshal now, eh?" said one.

"Yep, Joe. Been one for quite a spell. You sure been away a long time. And Bridger City is simply Satan's own loading pen now! A reg'lar broth is a-boiling there. Something fierce, I tell you. And Crosby down the line ain't but a few steps behind Bridger – though more under the surface."

"Can you whip that now? Well, who's rodding the Law down in Bridger now?"

"Adam Blair," said the other. "He's sheriff. You see, the county seat was switched to Bridger a little while after the railroad came in there. Yep, Blair. But the situation looks like she's too big for him too."

Red was galvanized despite his fatigue at mention of that name, the name of the man who'd killed his dad. It seemed as if it would crop up to haunt him forever. He steadied himself, prepared to go around and knock on the door and buy some grub. Then the one with the pipe finished lighting it and went on.

"Hear about that Red Paine, the outlaw's son? No? Shucks, man, you sure are ignorant. They're hunting him down this way now. He – hey, the java's boiling over!" He got up to go back to the kitchen.

And Red moved away from the window, knowing he couldn't go in there now, that he'd be recognized. Even if he jumped a gun on them, afterward they could spread the word he'd been there. He felt faint for a moment. He had been counting on getting some food so much. A faint whinnying came from the rear.

He slipped around there, sighted the shed with three ponies in it. When he was leading the dun horse out, one of the men opened the back door and flung away a pot of water. Red froze. But the door closed behind the gent. Pulling out his dinero, he counted off some bills. In his condition, he never was sure whether it was fifty or sixty. He got a stone and went back and left them in the shed where the dun had been, putting the stone atop them. Leading the horse to the woods, he worked around to where he'd left his own roan ground-anchored, switched the saddle to the dun. Leading the roan astride the "bought" cayuse, he swung in a wide loop around the cabin, hanging close to the fringe of trees, then followed the cart tracks on down the slope. A couple of miles on, he set the roan free in the woods. His spirits lifted a little.

Now he had a fresh mount, and the ponies

of the posses would be jaded, unless they'd managed to pick up new ones. Back there at the cabin, when they discovered the missing horse, they'd guess it had been his work. But that wouldn't be till tomorrow morning at least. Now, if he could only get some grub, he'd have a real chance. His head kept swimming from the faintness of semi-starvation. Sometimes he would find himself off in a dream, watching Harry Westfall's mouth work as he labored at tying that hated necktie again. Then he would catch himself slipping from the saddle with weariness.

The dawn grew from a pinkish lip on the eastern horizon, spread into a yellowish glow, began to lift the mantle of shadow from the earth. The damp of the ground mist touched his haggard face. He was in a tortuous canyon, riding beside the sere bed of a dried-up stream, slapping himself across the cheeks to rouse his dulled senses that shrieked for some shuteye.

The canyon angled sharply and at first he thought he had ridden into a settlement. It was right at the junction where the canyon divided into forks. There was a handful of shacks and hovels scattered back from the creek bed on each side. His gun was already in his hand as he peered through the shrouding mist. There was no sound. Then he saw the

105

paneless windows, the sagging doors, a porch leaning drunkenly, and realized it was a tiny little ghost town.

In the creek bed, shoulders hunched against the sudden wind that had whipped up from behind him, he rode through it. At the forks he wearily decided to take the one to the left. The wind soughed off the walls of the narrower branch canyon. He'd gone about a hundred yards up it when a party of horsemen rounded an elbow of rock in the other direction. Red whipped the dun around and fed the gut hooks to it, thus marking himself as a fugitive. But when he'd caught the faint gleam of the lawman's badge on the vest of the foremost rider, he had no alternative.

"Halt – Paine!" a shout came. A moment later, a bullet hissed over his low-bent body.

He guessed he had run smack into a third posse. From what he'd overheard back at that cabin, they were really scouring the country for him. The dun's hoofs rattled wildly on the loose stones of the canyon floor. Twisting once, Red flung a couple of blind shots back to slow down the pursuit if possible. He figured to turn into the other branch of the split canyon.

But it wasn't to be. Just as he started to swing the dun, its hoofs slipped on the dew-damp loose shale. Red flung himself

106

clear as the animal lurched, stumbled to its knees, then crashed heavily sideward into a big boulder. Red landed on all fours, forehead banging the ground. He was groggier when he scrambled up, and the horse was out of the picture, lying stunned a few yards away. Two slugs from that third posse ricocheted whiningly off nearby rocks. The outlaw's son ran back down the creek bed into the ghost town.

A drifting patch of ground mist saved him as he scrambled up one bank. But they sighted him again as, on weak legs, he stumbled into one of the abandoned hovels. He pushed past a drunkenly sagging door, almost collapsed from weakness and the crash he had taken. A wall caught him and he lay against it, trying to steel himself. He knew it would be his death trap. But he lacked the strength to try to duck out of it.

He moved over to where some loose boards had sagged at a corner of the place to leave an aperture. They had dismounted. They were coming along the old creek bank on that side toward him, seven of them led by the lawman, guns out. A few of them had rifles. They began to fan out.

"Paine, come out!" yelled the John Law. "You're trapped like a rat! You ain't got a chance. Come out – and live, fella."

The outlaw's son recalled the time on the bluff over Red Hat when he'd said about the same thing to a man. He stood silent.

The badge packer shifted over to get in a line behind a boulder. Watching, the man and the boulder alternately faded, then came clear again before Red's haggard eyes. The man called:

"Paine, we can ring that shack and fill you with lead inside uh five minutes! You know that. You wanta live longer than that, don't you? You're young yet. Why shake hands with the devil so soon? . . . Now come out with your hands on your hat, Paine!"

Red thought something stirred in the steamy air down behind the little bunch waiting there, but he put it down to the way his eyes were acting. He swallowed and snapped back:

"Come in and get me – you basted law dogs!"

The badge packer's voice became like a buckskin popper on a bull whip. "All right, boys. Ring the place an' then pour it into the blamed fool!"

This was it. This was the end of the trail for Big Red's boy – for all of the dead Big Red's own hopes. Red knew it. And though he had one foot on Boot Hill's doorsill, that last – his dad's hopes for him – seemed the more important. He saw one of them start down between a couple of cabins up there to swing around behind. And a moment later, Red saw the same man come staggering out and crumple down like an orey-eyed galoot going to sleep.

"Just freeze in your tracks – or be toted home with your boots on!" a new voice crackled on the rising day. A man, three more, rose like apparitions out of the creek bed a little way up from where the posse stood; appeared like angels of salvation straight from Heaven.

CHAPTER ELEVEN

It seemed like a veritable mirage at first. But there was the voice. Then the snarling whiplash of a gun as one of the law bunch jerked around too fast and the warning bullet chewed up earth close to him. That was the only shooting there was.

Caught from the rear, the posse pushed up their hands, guns thudding to the hard-packed earth as they were released. Only then did Red Paine realize what had happened to that man who'd reeled out after starting around the cabin up the line. He'd been dropped by one of them climbing out of the creek bed.

"Come on out, Paine. We're friends," called the leader, a towering gent, cadaverous face stubbled with black beard, half bald head gleaming in the rising light. He wore a pair of jeans, his undershirt, and was barefooted as if he'd been hastily aroused from bed.

"You're a danged lobo too," snorted the chagrined lawman.

"*Mi-ster* Lobo to you, badge packer. And –" And then he saw the lawman making a furtive play for the gun in the shoulder rig beneath his vest.

Red stepped onto the porch of the shack. It was one of the quickest plays Red had ever seen made. The slouching baldish man didn't jump or galvanize, didn't try to fling up the gun he held either. He just whipped a short eight-inch club from inside his belt. It chopped down. The lawman curled up on the baked mud with a little grunt. That was all. The big man stood smiling around as if extending a tacit invitation to any others, dangling the stick by a rawhide thong.

Red tottered down toward them. Things began to fade before him. He felt the big man's arms catch him, heard his rumble about letting Doc handle things. . . .

It was the sting of redeye in his throat that brought him out of the blackness. He found himself propped beside one of the ghost town hovels. Down in the creek bed the posse stood in the first sunlight, dew-claws over their heads. Another swig of whisky was worked between his lips. The fire of it strengthened him; but even then, the next moves were all very dream-like to him.

He saw one of the bunch leading a string of ponies out from the thickets behind the row of cabins on the opposite bank. In a vague way, he noted there were two extra horses. He was half lifted into the saddle of one. Then he saw the horses of the posse being brought over on a length of manila lead rope. The big gent with the black beard stubble waved cheerily to the whipped posse in the creek bed.

"We'll leave your cayuses 'bout ten miles up this branch, boys," he told them, pointing to the left fork of the canyon. "We wouldn't steal 'em. Shucks, they ain't very good ones anyway. All you gotta do is – walk to 'em. . . . *Adios*. No see long time – we hope." Chuckling, he led the way up the left fork.

The ride was very hazy to the outlaw's son. They stopped once and there was some hot java and he gulped down some chunks of jerked beef. After that he felt a little stronger when he got back in the hull. He heard one of the other three call the big baldish one Doc Sills. Red was spent, but the terrible stress of anxiety was removed. He felt among friends. And knew, feeling it, that they were outlaws.

They cut out of the canyon branch. He knew that because one of the others had to get at the bridle of his cayuse and tug to help it up the steep ribbon of shelf that switched-backed to the top. The sun was in mid sky when they rode into a big strip of mesquite jungle. Somebody said they'd stay there till nightfall. Hands helped Red out of the kak, lowered him to the ground gently. He rolled on his side, couched his head on a crooked arm, and sank into a deathlike sleep. Harry Westfall appeared in a dream in it and said he guessed Red wouldn't have to bother wearing a necktie any more. Harry looked like he'd bust out bawling when he said it.

When he pushed open his eyelids once more he looked straight up through a gap in the maze of grayish branches at icy-hued stars in the night sky. He heard the mutter of voices and pushed himself to a sitting position. The four of them were over around a tiny fire built in a hole scooped out of the sand. It threw almost no glow. A fat one with a big globe of sallow face rose from a hunkered-down position.

"Our friend, Red, is awake," he said, coming over.

The outlaw's son stopped knuckling his swollen eyes. "Say, how do you fellas know me?"

"Heard that dang posse yelling your name this morning," the fat man said, pushing the flannel shirt down inside his bulging jeans. "An' we'd learned the news they were curry-combing that whole piece of country for the deputy son of Big Red Paine. So-o –" He extended a hand to help Red as the latter struggled to get his stiff body to his feet.

"Howdy," he went on, pumping the hand he still held. "Me, I'm Bill Dornan, sometimes known as Laughing Bill." His affableness was plain. His mouth twitched as if to grin. His bright chips of blue eyes lighted pleasantly. But no actual smile came. Red was to learn Dornan had been dubbed "Laughing Bill" because he neither laughed nor smiled, ever.

Red found himself on guard slightly. "You knew my dad, I reckon." He was thinking of that other man, Ed Chess, who'd once known his dad.

Bill Dornan shook his head. Over at the fire, Doc Sills said no they hadn't. The other two shook their head also.

"But we know who – and what – he was," Dornan said. "We know he was one of the straightest, finest gents that ever answered an owl's hoot, kid."

"Thanks," Red said. He went over to the fire and met Doc Sills and the other two. One was Ed Rader, a handsome blond rannyhan, young, with overwide shoulders tapering down to a bullfighter's sleek hips. He was the only one who was shaven and all duded-out in fancy rig. A pair of white gauntlets hung looped over the silver-filigreed gunbelt he wore. The air he had told that he was aware just exactly how good-looking he was. The other was Pinch Morgrove, a little keyed-up man with sincere eyes and a nervous grin. He sort of bounced when he walked.

Red was handed a tin of coffee. He started to try to thank them for coming to his aid. Dornan pushed him brusquely and Doc Sills guffawed and told him to tie a bag over his head.

"That's a plumb instinctive thing with me, pardner, the saving of innercent young souls," Doc said. "Used to be a circuit-riding preacher up in Montana. Ran myself plumb ragged trying to stamp out sin." He made a descriptive snort, pulled at his long nose, and rumbled on. "It was a futile vocation, plumb futile. Sin, she's like grass, just keeps a-sprouting. And mankind is sure one fertile pastureland for it. Know what happened?"

Red found himself chuckling easily for the first time in many a long moon as he let Pinch Morgrove refill the can with java for him. He felt much better. And there was a warmth to the companionship about him, a warmth he'd never known since that last afternoon he'd ridden home from school. "No. What happened?" he asked.

Doc Sills lowered his head like a penitent but lost sinner. "I got plumb contaminated, infested, infected, and positively polluted with that sin myself. That's why I'm out here now, an owlhooter, associating with a pack of no-good buzzards like these here."

They all laughed but Rader. He just smiled, adjusting the knot of the silk neckerchief at his throat. Red got a quirly going. His wire-tough body seemed to renew its stamina minute by minute. After a spell, Dornan asked him about the accusation against him as deputy.

"You let that Powell out, eh?"

Red shook his head, in a few words telling them how it was. One of them clipped, "Good." They were outside the Law; but they too had no respect for a man who betrayed his own kind. Little Pinch brought the ponies in from a picket line.

"We'll hit out for the desert, huh, Doc?" said Dornan, pushing in a shirttail again.

Doc pulled his hat down over the front bald half of his head, nodded. "Reckon that's best, Bill."

Red gathered the two of them sort of split the authority. Then he spoke up, saying he was able to hit out alone if they'd lend him a pony. He said he didn't want them to get a catching because of him.

Doc said, "You go to blazes, Kid Red. . . . The posse ain't been born that can back-track me down in a piece of country I know."

They sloped out from the mesquite. In another hour, they dropped over a low rim and went down a rocky slope and onto the desert fringe. They rode the rest of the night, camped out of sight in a little clump of jackpine the next day. Pushing northward, two days later they reached a camp tucked up in a pothole in rough hill country they had used before. Doc told Red they'd pulled out of there a couple of weeks earlier and holed up at that ghost town, where Red stumbled upon them, to let things cool off. It seemed the handsome Ed Rader had gotten a mite orey-eyed and started a fracas in some pueblo up this way.

Rader scowled, cutting his eyes at Doc Sills from a lowered head. "That gopher called me

'Pretty Pete'. Was I going to let him get away with that?" He spat out an obscene string of oaths to answer his own query.

"Shooting up a place unnecessary-like is bad business for gents in our business," Dornan said. Rader walked away, cursing some more.

A few days later, Doc and Pinch Morgrove dropped down into the town on the creek to the north. When they returned that night, they had big news. They'd learned the stage from Donnelville would be coming through the next night with a big load of bank specie aboard.

Dornan wobbled his stub of black cigar across his yellow-skinned face. "Place to take it would be there afore she goes into the gulch." With a stick, he drew a map of the stage route in the dirt. "See, she comes down that steep hill, then has a turn sharp. Half a mile on, she goes into the gulch. They'll be ready for trouble there. But here, where she slows for the turn –" He stopped.

Red looked up and found four pairs of eyes on him. He read the unspoken question. Straightening from one knee, he cast the die. "Gents, if you can use an extra pair of guns, I tote 'em." *He was an outlaw!*

CHAPTER TWELVE

The stage hold-up went off as slick as hot grease. Red Paine knew what it meant for him, that he was committing himself practically irretrievably with this act. His conscience told him he was betraying his dad, but he argued it out with himself and told himself he wasn't. That if Big Red were there he would understand, would see that he had no alternative, no chance of riding on the other side of the fence now. Not with that Red Hat charge standing against him. He had tried to play it straight. Men wouldn't let him, riding him out of the herd because of the accident of his birth.

Little Pinch leaped out of the grass, yelling like mad and shooting his gun over the ponies' heads, as the coach maneuvered the curve with screeching brakes. The lead team shied. The skinner fought to hold them. The guard couldn't fire accurately from the lurching stage. Led by Doc, the others poured down the bank on their ponies at the other side of the road. Doc was alongside the front wheel and stretching from his saddle to crack that wooden club of his over the guard's head in a trice.

"Molly never fails me," he crowed as the guard tumbled over the wheel, his carbine rattling after him. "Molly" was his name for that effective stick of his. Red, closing like a whirlwind from behind, slammed a couple of shots through the coach roof to discourage any resistance as he came up on the other side.

They had the situation in hand inside of a minute. The skinner standing on the box, straining his arms toward the stars. The unconscious guard relieved of his side guns and checked for any hideout hardware. The three passengers, a drummer and two cowmen, lined up beside the stage.

But there was no bank specie aboard. The only freight was a trunk and a small packing case. When they were banged open, the trunk revealed it was stuffed with clothes. In the packing case was simply an order of pots and pans addressed to some general store. One of the cowmen had almost seventy dollars. The other rancher, so drowsy with redeye he could scarcely stand, had a bank order, a few dollars in silver. The masked road agents exchanged glances. It was a bitter disappointment, a poor showing for the risk of their hides. Dornan, going over the trembling drummer, came up with twenty dollars from inside one of his shoes.

"Let him keep it," Doc said. "The poor devil's got to travel to earn his living. . . . See if there's anything inside."

Pinch Morgrove bounded inside. Red caught a faint scraping. Standing by one of the rear wheels, stepped back, looked up along beside the coach. The knockedout guard, lying in the grass, was coming to. He had started to sit up. Then the Colts of Rader lifted up front and the guard wrenched back into the grass with a wounded arm.

"You dang idiot!" roared Doc.

Another minute and they were back in the saddle, cutting away from the road and getting the devil out of there. Back at the camp, nobody felt very good about it. A jug of redeye was produced. The four sat around the fire taking swigs from it. Red stood off by a tree, coldly furious inside. Then Rader muttered:

"Jumping Jupiter! That skinner had a big fat gold watch chain. Probably a dang good watch at the end of it too. I remember seeing it, then forgetting it 'cause we were going to get the specie." He spat into the fire. "I'd like to go back there and bend a gun barrel over his head, by grab! He's probably laughing like anything now thinking how we missed it!"

That was too much for Red. Pinching out his quirly, he strode over. "Shooting that isn't necessary is plain chunk-headed business," he said slowly.

When Ed Rader looked up and found the gray eyes locked on him, he put the jug down and stood up slowly. He was a good forty pounds bigger than the slim Red. "You got a big mouth for a little greenhorn," he said.

Red walked unhurriedly around the fire to face him. All he could think of was how the crazy trigger finger of a member of his dad's outfit had eventually cost Big Red Paine his own life. He let his eyes run over Rader.

"That guard was stripped of his shooting irons. You knew that. He was helpless. Putting a hole in him wasn't necessary. It's fool stuff like that that brings the Law down hard on you. . . . Sometimes you kill a man, then you get all the country on your coat tails."

"Now, fellas," said Bill Dornan, jumping up as he stuffed in a shirt end. "Now –"

Rader swelled out his big chest and spat into the fire. "Mebbe some gents is so lily-livered, a spot of blood scares 'em outa their britches, huh? This is a rough game. If you ain't got sand in your craw –"

Red cut in with, "It takes a fighting fool, I reckon, to slam lead into an unarmed man. . . .

Or maybe a danged scared fool!"

Rader yelped an obscene name and swung his big arm, and Red Paine was on him like a wildcat, driving a hurricane of blows. Hit once, he bounced off a tree. He rushed, smashed Rader's jaw. Rader thudded to the earth. He wasn't out cold. He sat up after a few moments, eyes lighted with a venomous glow.

"Want any more?" Red asked. "Or maybe you'd rather try it some other way." He tapped one of his ivory butts.

Radar stood up and rubbed at some blood on his fancy silk shirt. He shook his head in sullen, black wrath. Dorman offered the jug.

"Red's right about the gunning, Ed. . . . And you got what you asked for. Now, let's have a drink all around and forget it, huh?"

Ed Rader sneered and went into the lean-to.

"You got the plumb fastest hands I ever saw, Red," Doc Sills told him with a new note of respect in his voice.

It was toward the end of that week that Doc Sills came back from traipsing around and reported a new gambling hall down in Donnelville. He said the place was doing a heap big business, and that they employed only two house guards. It was decided to take it a few days later when the furore over the stage hold-up would have died down.

"We can bust out the north side of the town, hit over that stretch of sand dunes, then loop around this way," Doc figured it.

"All right," Dornan agreed. "Only if we're a-going to stay in this camp that much longer, we'll need some fresh grub."

Rader offered to go in and get it. There was a little store down the creek before a man reached that next town. It made it unnecessary for any of them to go into the town where he might get grabbed. Rader left the next morning, promising to bring back some cigars for Laughing Bill.

The day wore away slowly, lazily. Sometimes Red thought of his dad. But he felt he would understand. Doc Sills gave himself a shave and told about the days when he'd peddled patent medicine from the tailboard of a wagon with a travelling show after giving up the calling of the Lord. He said he used to die laughing how folks would buy a bottle, take a swig, and claim they felt better in a few minutes. He told them it was a secret Injun recipe. But he used to make up fresh batches late at night after the show closed down. It was just some colored water with some herb juice, plus a good jolt of redeye and the taste killed with licorice flavoring.

"Old ladies and parsons seemed to like it

best of all," he guffawed.

At sunset, Bill Dornan, who did the cooking, was fretting around. Rader should have been back by mid-afternoon. Then the handsome Ed rode in, bragging about the pretty filly with red hair he'd met in the store and how he'd sparked around her for a while. He was in high spirits, said he couldn't wait till they got to visit with her again.

On the second day after that, they saddled up with the dawn still a gray promise to ride for Donnelville. Rader turned down all the grub at breakfast, saying he felt sick. He had pains in his belly, he said. After a couple of hours riding, he dropped from the saddle and writhed on the ground, cursing the cramps gripping his insides. He gave Bill Dornan some dirty looks as if it might be the result of his grub. At dusk, they were on a wooded promontory outside the town, watching the main street, burning down quirlies. Rader sat propped against a tree, alternatively groaning and cursing.

Finally, Pinch Morgrove rode in alone to look things over. He was a good man for the job because, being small and insignificant in appearance nobody noticed him much. Nobody would recall seeing him afterward. An hour later he returned to report that everything seemed set, looked normal. The

124

evening stage had pulled out. The town marshal had closed up his office and gone home; Pinch had followed him almost to his doorstep. The gambling hall was swinging into a big night of action.

They waited another hour. Doc stomped out his quirly and said, "Let's go in and beat the game." They moved toward the well-rested ponies; they had ridden easy on the way over. Then Rader staggered back as he lifted a foot to the stirrup. He said he just couldn't make it, he felt like he was poisoned.

"I'll wait here for you fellas," he said, grimacing and holding his belly. "If you can't git back this way, don't worry. I'll manage somehow. Mebbe after I lie down a spell. . . ."

They finally left him, walked their ponies along the main road to the edge of town, sized it up. There had to be a slight change in the plans. Originally Pinch was to have stayed outside with the ponies, prepared to cover them when they busted out with the dinero. But now he'd come in with them; it would take four men. Doc was nervous, admitting he had a hunch, an uneasy feeling. They sat there in the soft warm night for a spell.

"Reckon I might go home after this," Pinch mentioned. "Just for a little visit.

I got that widowed sister you know over in the Territory. She's got a coupla fine young boys. One of 'em sorta looks like me." His voice took on a wistful note. "Me, I never had no children of my own.... Wife took sick and died six months after we was married."

"Sure, that'll be all right, Pinch," Dornan said, working his mouth around the cigar stub.

They rode in and left their ponies ground-anchored in the shadow of a tree at a closed store across the road from the gambling hall. They ambled by its brightly lighted interior once. Everything looked normal. The baize-topped tables seemed to be doing a fair business. They saw the roulette wheel further back. Doc said the boss sat on a high stool at the end of the bar. Right beside him was the door to his office. The dinero was kept in the safe there. They had rehearsed the details.

They crossed the street. Pinch Morgrove eased into the alley to get down to the side door. They gave him a few seconds, then sauntered up the wide steps and in the front. Red had the strange feeling it was too easy as they passed one house guard by the door. The other, a fat owlish man, lolled over by the side wall. Pinch would have him covered. Unhurriedly they walked along the bar, Dornan dropping back a little. Red and Doc were to take the boss. They hesitated when they saw he wasn't on the stool.

"He'll be around soon and –" Doc was whispering.

Then three gents just down the bar whirled suddenly. The stubby one wore the town marshal's badge. The trio of outlaws there were looking at three drawn guns. From the tail of his left eye, Red saw several men rise from card tables at the side of the room, swinging up Colts they'd been holding drawn beneath the table tops.

They'd walked into a trap, no question of it. Somebody tipped off the Law. Must have even described them pretty well.

"Nice evening, ain't it, gents?" drawled the town marshal sarcastically. "Push your dewclaws up to that ceiling now!" He nodded at Red. "Paine the double-crossing deputy, ain't it?"

Though his gray eyes had that stony shine, Red Paine managed a smile, the sad smile of a man who knows he's whipped. But he kept on walking. He was the hombre who might as well be dead as captured. He knew this somehow was a double-cross job. And that cold lashing thing was going inside him. "Marshal, my hat's off to you. You're danged smart. Now how –"

Then he was right in front of the gloating town marshal. Red sort of lifted his hands out before him as if offering him the opportunity to get his guns. But with that incredible speed he possessed in those hands, he did the unexpected with sudden swiftness. No draw. He simply smashed the marshal in the jaw with his right hand. The next instant, his left beat down on the marshal's gun, forcing the muzzle floorward.

It was the last move anybody would have expected. The marshal was staggered back against the bar. Red leaped and clutched him and wheeled him around to put his body between himself and the room. With that same blinding speed, he snaked out his own smokepole and jabbed it in the marshal's side just as a gunshot thundered in the place.

"Hold those triggers!" Red called: "Hold 'em – or the marshal gets it!" He saw the two who'd been at the bar with the marshal standing there goggle-eyed and hesitant. Pulling his Colts from the law officer's side an instant, Red slashed at the forearm of one and knocked his weapon clattering to the floor.

Doc was in action, slicking out Molly, his club. The next instant, the third one was gunless and shrieking with the agony of his battered forearm. Dornan leaped up, his two bared weapons wheeling over the place. And then, across the room, over by the side door, they saw that little Pinch half bent over a table, holding his side. One of the gents who'd helped to make this trap had cut down on him just as he stepped in and Red made his play for the marshal.

Nothing happened for moments. The room was like some frozen scene, petrified by the cold nerve and daring and terrible swiftness of the outlaw's son. "Gawd, the speed of you!" Doc muttered despite the peril of the situation.

And Red Paine was master of that situation. He saw little Pinch straighten, wave that he would be all right. Red, eyes cutting around, incredibly possessed despite his youth, said dryly:

"All right, we're leaving. And we're taking the marshal along a ways just for a quiet ride in the moonlight. *Sabe?*" Under the high-curled hat brim his face was a calm mask. "Quiet – so long as nobody follows us. Try it – and the marshal has his last ride ... *Last*, I said! ... Bill, help Pinch over." Red was the boss then.

It worked. They backed out, Red jerking the marshal along with them. They picked up a pony from the gambling hitchrail for him, got in their own saddles across the road, hedged him in, rode out the way they'd come. Pinch held his hand against his wounded side but sat his kak all right. He said he thought he'd been drilled between the ribs. Nobody said anything else.

They went up the road and swerved off to the promontory where they'd left Ed Rader. He was gone. Then they knew who the double-crosser had been, who'd sold them out. . . .

CHAPTER THIRTEEN

Some miles on, back in a little draw, they cut the cinch strap of the town marshal's saddle, then let him go. The tubby man rode off cursing and promising vengeance, but he was soon forgotten completely as the wounded Pinch began to feel worse. They had already strapped a wadded piece of his shirt over the slash between his ribs, but it didn't seem to staunch the blood flow. And he had a paleness like gray snow that was thawing from the bottom.

They gave him several slugs of redeye and

wadded a neckerchief too over the wound. From all appearances, it seemed the slug had passed out at the back of the side. Little Pinch tried to treat it lightly. But his eyes had a haunted look. He mentioned that widowed sister of his again. And then, when they were halfway back to the camp on the stretch of sand, he sort of slid down from the kak before Dornan could catch him and stood holding himself erect with his grasp on the saddle horn.

"I'm slowing you fellas down," he said. "It might mean a catchin'. Mebbe you better go ahead."

They refused, of course. Another look at the wound showed it still bled steadily. On a flesh gash the blood should have clotted and encrusted by then. Red stepped off with Doc and told him he thought it was internal bleeding. That perhaps the bullet had struck bone, and a broken segment of the lead had plunged deeper into the body. He asked where the nearest sawbones was.

"They's one at the edge of the town up the creek from the camp. 'Course – dang it, we can take the chance for Pinch." What he meant was that going there meant risking capture. The doctor would suspect strangers bringing in a shot-up man at that hour of the night.

They cut back down to the stage road. Now Pinch was too weak to keep himself in the kak. He rode double with Red, the smallest of the other three, clutching him from behind. It was just as Dornan announced they had only about four more miles that Pinch's contorting hands clutched at Red's ribs, fell away. When they lifted him to the ground, he was wax-colored with his eyes sunken back in his head. Once he grinned up feebly, closed his eyes. Red put his leather-hued cheek close to the open mouth. There was no breath.

They buried little Pinch at the base of a big gaunt pine off the trail. Doc said Pinch always used to say that when he had a home he'd build it under the biggest pine he could find around. He said they gave him a feeling of being closer to Heaven. When they'd finished piling rocks atop the grave to balk the coyotes, Bill Dornan told Doc to say something.

"You should remember a real prayer – like from the book." Dornan had tears streaming unashamedly down his cheeks. For once he paid no heed to a shirt tail that hung out in front.

Doc said, "Nothing in the book's good enough for Pinch." Then: "Take him, Lord. Treat him easy. Pinch was a good one, a real good one."

Red walked away, building a tube of Durham. He hadn't known Pinch long, but he'd come to be very fond of the keyed-up, gentle, little man always willing to help another. He couldn't help but have a big chunk of respect for any hombre who was afraid but went ahead anyway. And Ed Rader, conceited about his looks but with a yellow stripe inside, had done this. Done it because he wanted to pay back the man who'd revealed that stripe, Red himself.

"Think he'll be back at the camp?" Red asked.

Doc shook his head. "He's lit out. Once he saw we weren't trapped in that gambling hall, he put his foot in his hand and made tracks."

They didn't say anything for a spell. There was a gurgle when Bill Dornan took a drink from the bottle. Red kicked dust.

"All right. I'm a young jasper. I got plenty of years to find him. I will." Red put on his hat.

Doc Sills looked at Molly in his hand. "You ain't going to be riding alone on that job, Red. Is he, Bill?"

Dornan wiped his mouth thoughtfully. "Wait a minute ... I remember Rader mentioning once he had a married brother who was a barkeep over in Bridger City. You know, I got a hunch he'd headed for

133

there.... Only trouble is, Ed's real handle wasn't Rader. Still ..."

"That Judas Iscariot! He didn't have much dinero in his jeans, I know ... Yes, he'd run for Bridger, I'm thinking. And if he's there, we'd be bound to spot him sooner or later. Sooner, I hope. 'Cause when I was in Donnelville last week, I heard that Jud Tentrus was heading back to Bridger as a special gun marshal. Tentrus, they tell, resigned from the Federal service."

"I thought Adam Blair was the sheriff there now," Bill said.

"Still is," agreed Doc. "But it seems some kind of special citizens' committee is hiring Tentrus to come in. And you know how he's poison to our breed." He spat. "Bridger's less 'n two days ride from here."

Red Paine stood silent. Adam Blair, the man who'd killed his dad, who'd be a sworn enemy of his. And Tentrus, whom he'd vowed to break some day, who believed an outlaw spawned an outlaw.... To ride into their bailiwick....

He walked over and swung aboard his cayuse. "What're we waiting for, a special invitation?"

They came out of a pass between jagged peaks and followed a road that worked steadily

134

southward, sloping and dropping in sharp dips down from the hills that served the peaks as footstools. The afternoon wore on, a lead-vaulted sky seeming to cramp the heat down, impish gusts of wind slapping waves of alkali into their sweaty faces. They had to ride with neckerchiefs up over their noses and mouths, and Red Paine had an eerie feeling, a sensation of having been there before.

He had done a heap of thinking as they'd worked toward Bridger to track down the polecat who'd sent them into that Donnelville trap that had killed poor Pinch. Always, like an invisible cloud of guilt over him, was the idea he was betraying his dad. He couldn't shake it off. Yet he knew the owlhoot he now forked had been a choice thrust on him, that men wouldn't let him ride the other side of the fence as hard as he had tried. Still the decision he had made haunted him. He felt there were two Red Paines inside him struggling for possession of his life. He had a split feeling. But he did know that what he was now doing, seeking to cut the sign of a double-crosser, his dad would have approved of.

Doc Sills had talked some about this big seething cauldron of a range town. He said there was a certain cautiously whispered mystery about it. That men rode into Bridger and dropped from sight as if into a bottomless pit. They just never were seen again. Nobody heard anything about them.

"But, according to the whispers," Doc said, "they weren't killed. I heard a man once call 'em the living dead, but he was scared to say anything more than that." John Laws coming in after wanted men they knew were in Bridger just vanished. A special investigator sent down from the state capital was never heard from again. Three more were sent in to find him. They suddenly left Bridger without explaining why. Doc had heard of two separate cases where wire-tough gents had hit the town to avenge friends they believed killed there. They did no avenging. They'd just dragged their tails out sheepishly.

And the strangest part of it was that Bridger had Law and plenty of it. There was the sheriff, Adam Blair, who'd built himself a rep as a hell-fire-and-brimstone deputy before coming to Bridger. As if that weren't enough, there was a powerful Vigilante organization to act as an extra arm of the Law.

"And it's a real outfit, they tell," Doc assured them as they rounded a bend past a stand of yellow pine. He shot Red a look.

Again Red Paine had that uncanny sensation of somehow knowing this road.

"A real outfit," Doc repeated. "It's

membership is even a secret. Nobody knows who is and who isn't a Vigilante. Yet the wave of lawlessness goes on like a terrible flood." Hold-ups were common. Men were murdered in alleys for a few dollars. The two banks were busted into. Stages were stopped out on the trails. There were train robberies. Blood flowed in Bridger almost like water. "Somebody in there is bigger than the Law itself, I tell you."

Crosby, a lesser town some miles down the big valley from Bridger, was a quieter, smaller edition. For years, before Bridger had gone bad, Crosby had been its sort of underworld, its Whisky Row, a salty pueblo with little law, a place where a wanted man on the run knew he could be taken care of and hidden. Now, according to some of the whispers on the out-trails and along the owlhoot, they were connected, both a part of some invisible empire.

"Me, I'm wanted in one state and got charges against me in a couple of counties," Doc admitted, pulling at his long nose. "When I get my light put out, I doubt I'll be associating with the seraphim or cherubim up there. And I won't exactly get deaf from hearing the strumming of the angels' harps up there." He lifted his head toward heaven.

"Never cared for harps much anyway. But this –" he jerked his head in the direction of Bridger " – this is plum pure evil! . . . Mebbe I should've settled down with a good woman in my younger years. It was riding that soul-saving trail that ruined me."

Red didn't grin. The mention of a woman made him think of that copper-haired girl, Peg, who'd twice saved his hide. For some reason, he had been remembering her often of late, thinking how her voice sounded, how her hair had looked in pigtails that time. The quiet poised courage of her. Then he lifted his head, squinting against the fierce sunlight. And his heart seemed to bounce into his throat.

Thirty odd yards ahead was a little bridge spanning a small ravine. As they neared, he saw the creek down in the bottom of the ravine. It was where he and Ed Chess had hidden that time Tentrus and his posse had been hounding them after the attempted holdup of that dancehall, where they had parted company with Chess. Then he understood the queer sensation of seeming to know this trail. He had been on it before. Bridger City was the town where, that terrible night, Jud Tentrus had almost beaten off his head in the jailhouse.

For a moment a chill hit him. That

night, Tentrus had gun-whipped him because Tentrus wouldn't believe the son of an outlaw wasn't lying. But if Tentrus should get his hands on him now as a prisoner again with that charge of being the crooked deputy of Red Hat against him. . . .

The chill passed. And a quiet sure premonition possessed the outlaw's son. Adam Blair was sheriff here. Tentrus had returned or was on his way back. It was like a lot of loose strings being twisted to a head. And for a purpose of Fickle Fate's. The purpose – a pay-off showdown . . .

CHAPTER FOURTEEN

Entering the big bustling town that seemed to wax fat on its crime and violence, Red remembered their mission: to get that Judas named Ed Rader. He pushed his own emotions into the background as they rode down the side street where that same dancehall Chess had tried to jump stood. They turned into a tree-fringed lane that ran behind the buildings of the main line, passed through a squalid section of shacks and hovels pushing out onto the sage flats to the west, then cut down a wide alley. They had decided to ask no questions. In Bridger, that could be dangerous. It would be just a matter of dogging the whisky mills and honky tonks till they came upon either Rader or his brother. Dornan said Rader had let on once his brother and he looked a heap alike.

Leaving their ponies under a tree down by that end of the main street where the alley came in, they started along the broken wooden sidewalk. The long-bodied, half-bald Doc Sills. The fat, yellowish-skinned Laughing Bill Dornan with the charred chunk of cigar sitting restlessly in his mouth. And the lean black-haired Red Paine, almost mild-looking save for the gray eyes that could turn to fire-backed stones. Across the wide main road, a little street straggled off down a rocky grade. Part way down it, a sign spiked out from a little building reading "Barroom". Red made a motion with his head. They moved over and down toward it.

It was a mangy little dive, the paint peeling from its clapboard front with the mixed aroma of stale beer and tobacco smoke hitting them in the face as they pushed through a swarm of green flies at the door. Doc put on an act at once, guffawing loudly as if he'd just heard a joke and whacking Red on the back. There was danger enough Rader might spot them appearing too obviously on the prowl for somebody. After the strong sunlight it took them a moment to, get accustomed to the dimness of the interior. At that hour, there was only a single customer, an old saloon tramp dozing at the front of the bar.

Then the bar boss came climbing out of a chair tilted back in a corner, rubbed his face with a greasy apron the while he yawned as he moved behind the counter. The apron was lowered. And the trio thought at first they were looking at Ed Rader himself.

Fortune seemed to have dealt them an ace with the first card. This man was not duded out like Ed, and he had a snaky little red scar running back into the hair by one temple. But it was plainly Ed Rader's brother. Bill Dornan made a choking sound, then threw away his cigar stub as if to blame it on that. That was the only sign they gave. Doc called for three drinks.

"All we got to do now is wait," he remarked casually. The other two knew what he meant. Either Ed Rader would come in to see his brother or, sooner or later, this brother would have to go home. Of course there was always the possibility that Ed the Judas had not come to Bridger.

Somebody called, "Alf," and Rader's brother went back and into a hallway that ran along one side of the low-ceiled long building. Doc began to whistle something that sounded like a funeral dirge. Red sauntered across the room of the bare place. The shutters of a window on the side were loosely pulled together and he casually poked one open a few inches for a looksee. A bare lot of rank grass with tin cans and debris scattered through it behind the line of trees in the front stretched on that side. Glancing rearward, he saw that the barroom building had an unsuspected ell in the rear that ran behind the high grass of the lot. About to turn away, he looked to the rear again. There were a few grimy windows on the front side of the ell back there.

Through one of them he could see two figures seated across a table arguing. The one to the left was slight and almost boyish-looking despite the black sombrero jammed low on his forehead. The other, burly with a heavy mustache, was starting to rise, hand dropping toward a gun butt. One of the window panes was out. And a moment after a rider passed up the side road, the outlaw's son caught their voices.

The burly one was saying, "I don't give a hoot what you say, button! You're the one who robbed me that night last week down in Crosby, ya dirty coyote! Now, you can give me back my dinero —"

142

"You're locoed," the slight one's voice came through the window hole. "Take me up to the sheriff. I'm not afraid. I –"

Up on the main line a wagon rattled by and Red lost the rest. But he blinked twice; it was impossible. Still, that low voice –

It was then a movement inside a window to the left of the other caught his eye. He saw it was a room between the other and the main building, a room behind the slight figure still in the chair. The movement was that of a man. And then Red saw the drawn gun in his hand, saw him cautiously inching open a door behind the sitting figure.

"I git back my dinero, ya coyote, or they's going to be some gunpowder burnt!" the burly one in the first room barked, hooking a hand to his gunbelt.

The mustached one guffawed sharply. "Aw right ya rat! Now gimme my dinero back – or draw!" He straightened, hands lifted in front of him, out away from his guns, as if encouraging the other to make a play.

Red recognized the trick. He'd heard his dad speak of it angrily. Tricked into thinking he had a chance, the other would draw. Then, the gent hidden at his back would send a bullet through the flesh of his gun arm before he could fire. And the first hairpin would unhurriedly kill the poor devil with a

143

shot from in front. It would never look like a drygulching job, yet it was. When the dead man would be found, he apparently had drawn, been winged through the arm and shot down.

Jabbing the shutter wider, in a split second Red had a gun nose through the opening. It spurted muzzle flame twice. Window glass was shattered in the second room where the drygulcher crouched at the door. Red saw him tilt over against the wall, hit. Red tried to throw the shutter wider to get out but something jammed it.

"What's the matter?" Dornan yelled.

"Friend of mine," called Red, running for a door in the back of the barroom. He kicked it open, both ivory-stocked guns out and cocked. The room was empty save for a table and a rumpled cot. But on the right a door led to the ell that jutted out there. As Doc Sills pounded in at his back he yanked that door open. It was the room where the drygulcher had been crouched. There were a few drops of blood on the floor beside an open window at the rear of the room that told its own story. Red barely gave them a glance as he rushed on toward the next room where the pair had been arguing.

He hit the ajar door with his shoulder, then dropped to a knee. But no volley of lead flamed his way. The burly hombre had cleared out too. And the slight one in blue jeans and shirt stood half sagging over the table, clutching a gun in one gloved hand. There was the dent of a gun-barrel blow in the black hat on the bowed head.

"Get me out – quick – if you can," the slight one said weakly. "They'll come back – only more of them. . . . They've marked me for death." Then the figure in blue started to crumple.

Red caught the slim body in an arm. The stout Dornan moved around Red and lifted the body from him. "If this is a pard of yours, Red –"

Even as Red nodded the level-headed Doc said, "We got to git outa here pronto, gents. Shooting makes so danged much noise it always brings the tin badgers nosing around."

They knew that. None of them, particularly Red, could afford to meet up with the Law. Few words were required among them. They functioned like a team, steady calm men who remained that way even under fire. To go back through the barroom might invite even more trouble. Red indicated the window on the street side of the ell with a gun barrel. Shoving it up, he slid out, turned to watch for trouble that might come through the screen of high grass and weeds. Doc was next. Dornan passed him the unconscious figure, followed.

Up at the front of the lot, Doc said matter-of-factly, "We don't know where we're going. The ponies'd come in handy. Cover me, Red." They stepped out through the thick saplings, leaving Dornan supporting the unconscious button. Moving swiftly but without any sign of panic, the two went up the grade. Doc ducked behind a freighter's wagon to the alley where the ponies were. Some men were already starting down that way. When the first rounded the corner store, he almost bumped into Red lounging against it. Red had his arms folded across his chest, the muzzle of the Colts in his right hand poking suggestively from under the left elbow. He asked in a bored voice:

"What's the matter, friend? Looking for somebody?"

The man sort of pulled back from the impact of those grey eyes. He said there'd been some shooting down there.

"Just some orey-eyed pelican gone trigger-loco," Red said coldly. "You wouldn't want to go down there and get hurt — or *would* you?" The man sort of stammered, retreated another step as some others turned into the path down the street. "Why don't you gents wait till the Big Law himself comes along? Those are my orders?"

A tall red-faced man blurted, "Are you a deputy?"

Red switched his eyes to him lazily. "Adam Blair told me I didn't have to answer to anybody but him, mister."

The mention of the name was like magic. Doc came through with the ponies. Red hooked his finger to the tall gent. "Keep everybody out till the sheriff comes along, will you?"

"Danged right!" said the man enthusiastically, hooking out a gun and facing the gathering throng. He was honored by the selection of himself for the job. "Now you heard the Law's orders! Ever'body, back there or I'll wrap this around somebody's ear, by grab!"

Red trotted down the slope to where the ponies were by the saplings. Doc swung up and reached to prop the half-stirring figure in blue across the saddle before him. Then Dornan and Red were mounted. Strangely, nobody had so much as poked his nose out of the barroom. Another moment and they were moving off on down the straggling street at a stiff trot. It angled sharply after passing a boarded-up house. Another hundred yards and it was just a broad dusty path between high weeds leading out into the heavy scrub growth.

"Handle her as easily as you can, Doc," Red said.

"Her?"

"It's a woman, Doc."

CHAPTER FIFTEEN

In another five minutes, like a gift from heaven, the rain came. The lead sky had darkened, swallowed the sun; then the water came down in sheets, obliterated all trail sign, hanging a veritable curtain between them and the town. It gushed down in roaring rivulets in the sand among the scrub growth. In a matter of minutes, the pony hoofs made sucking soughing sounds when they came out of the drenched ground. The rain slashed into their eyes, blinding them for seconds at a time. And it helped to revive the girl. Once she cried out and tried to struggle from Doc's long arms.

Then they swung off to get under the protection of a big eucalyptus plus a wedge of outcropping lava. Red helped the girl down to the ground and laid her close to the rock, placing Dornan's ragged, rusty black coat over her. She made a vague gesture at rubbing the bump on her head where the gunman had struck her with his Colts. And after another minute, her eyes remained open and began to focus. She jerked in surprise at sight of Red.

"Red Paine," she gasped. "How did you – how –"

"I might ask you the same thing, Miss Peg," he said. "How did you get here? But just take it easy now."

"Sure, ma'am. There isn't anything to worry about now." Doc put in. "Why –"

But she struggled up to the knees of her now wetted and muddied blue jeans. She clutched at the black sombrero that had slipped from her head. It revealed the fact that her copper-colored hair had been cropped off short like a man's, was parted to one side. Despite their predicament, Red felt himself growing a little angry about that. The sheen of that luxuriant hair was something he had always remembered about her.

"We've got to go – to keep going," she babbled a little wildly. "You don't know them ... They – they're everywhere. They'll find me again. They –" She even beat at Doc as he tried to stop her from rising.

"Who're they?" Red asked gently, putting an arm about her narrow waist to steady her as she swayed.

"I don't know," she said wearily. She

sounded out of her head. Dornan made a sign that she was.

"Nobody's going to get you now," Red tried to tell her. "There're three of us with you. We'll –"

She jerked away from him impatiently. "You don't know them. They just tried to kill me because, somehow, they suspect I've learned too much. I haven't – not yet. But perhaps –" She pushed a lock of the hair off her forehead and readjusted her sombrero. Suddenly she was very calm. "Please. Believe me, I'm not just a delirious female. Look – I can show you how to get up to my cabin outside town. There, we'll be safe – if anybody can be in Bridger – for a while."

She sounded very rational then. Red gave the signal. They mounted in the rain, this time the girl riding double with Red himself. He could feel her behind him on the cayuse, feel her hand on his shoulder. He steeled himself at first; then it was a nice feeling. At her direction, they began to bear westward, moving out of the stretch of sage and sand. The torrential downpour was already thinning.

Swinging in a loop around Bridger as the train whistled emerging from the cut outside the other end of the cowtown, they crossed the main trail, entered a small draw. She was cool and possessed now as she guided them. And a short while later, up on the side of a low hill, they passed a huge boulder to come out on the level space at the end of the path that led to the cabin there.

Inside, Dornan got a fire going in the sheet-iron stove while the girl retired to the bedroom behind to change her clothes. It was strange, Red thought, how destiny operated. Now another of the loose string ends had been brought in with the others. Because vengeful Ed Rader, when he'd gone down to the creek store, had slipped on into town and tipped the Law off to their plans, and the local lawman had passed the word on to Donnelville, they had hit here on Rader's trail, and practically stumbled over this girl he'd never expected to see again. When he'd watched the scene in the ell, he'd been almost certain it was she because of that controlled yet vibrant quality of her voice, a voice he'd never forgotten since that first awful night here in Bridger. And now . . .

She emerged in fresh clothing. But she still wore a pair of jeans, though she'd removed the gloves she wore as part of her masculine disguise. She smiled at them. "My name is Peggy Dana," she said.

"Peggy Dana," Red said under his breath. It had a nice sound to it, a sort of rhythm.

Then he remembered himself and made the introductions all around.

"You're all outlaws, I imagine," she said.

Dornan almost lost his cigar at the calm way she said it. Doc Sills bowed. "At your service, miss. But in the future, kindly refer to us as knights of the sage."

Then there was an awkward silence after a chuckle, and nobody seemed to know what to say. She turned from a window.

"There's no way I can really thank you. Words are so little ... The only thing I can do is to warn you – warn you to leave here now, after what you did for me. You're marked. Sooner or later they'll catch up to you. Then ..." She shook her head with a resigned, helpless air.

Dornan said they didn't scare easy. She whipped around on him.

"There've been others who didn't either. Nobody's seen them in a long time ... Once they get after you –" Again she shook her head.

"Who's this 'they?'" Doc asked.

She shrugged. "If I only knew ... I've been trying to find out. But ..." She made a helpless gesture. Silence settled again.

Red was watching her closely. Indeed, it was hard for him to drag his eyes away from this girl. He asked bluntly, "That night in the dancehall, when I was on the run from Red Hat as an accused deputy, why did you warn me? You saved me here at the jail that time, earlier. Then . . ."

She met his gaze. "I don't know," she said frankly. "I – I just didn't think you were the breed who double-crossed."

"Even though I'm an outlaw's son?"

"Yes . . . I just thought . . ." Then a slow flush stained her cheeks. Red felt the blood storm into his face as their eyes locked. Something like a current leaped between them in the little cabin. A woman confesses something deep when she admits to believing in an unknown man with all the signs against him.

Red went on quietly after a moment, though he sucked on his quirly hard again and again. He told her their game, why they had come to Bridger. He gave her their confidence though Dornan looked as if he didn't like it too much. But it broke the ice, caused her to lower her guard. He ended, "And if he should make tracks out of here, I reckon you should too." He told her about the killer crouched at the door in the room behind her in the ell.

Seating herself, she nodded. "Yes, I knew it was a game to kill me. That yarn of the one with the mustache about robbing him in Crosby was just a windy, of course. A man on the street told me to go down there to meet Joe ... I often met him there ... When I saw Joe wasn't there, I knew there was something wrong, that they'd learned something – discovered, perhaps, I knew too much. They didn't seem to know I was a woman, though."

"Who is this 'they?" Doc asked again.

Again Peg Dana shook her short-cropped head. "That is what I've been trying to find out for a long time, trying so hard." She looked at the glowing stove and her eyes seemed reddish a moment in the reflected light. Then she shifted slightly so she faced the standing Red Paine. "My father was one of the men who disappeared so mysteriously here. That was almost two years ago. I – I've been trying to find him."

She went on, her voice low, the emotion behind it held under a tight rein. Her father, Matt Dana, she told them, was a retired lawman himself. But he had strapped on his pistols and left home once more when one of his best friends was killed in Bridger City, a deputy chasing a denizen of the place. He'd come to Bridger, and sunk from sight.

"Killed too, I reckon," said Doc.

She shook her head, making a motion to smooth a skirt over her knees, then remembering she wore jeans. "No, that's it.

154

We got a note in his handwriting, Mother and I. It told us to do nothing, that he was alive but couldn't return home. And we've been paying ransom ever since, a hundred or so every so often. We had to sell our home. We got word at intervals that unless we pay some more Dad will die. That's why I came to Bridger in the beginning."

Nobody interrupted her. It was a compelling, strange, almost unbelievable story. She'd come and tried to locate her father. It was a hopeless game. Then, grimly, she had decided to try to solve the whole thing, to trace down the man behind this thing in vicious violent Bridger, a town that had gone bad since Jud Tentrus had departed it.

First she had worked as a waitress in an eating place, listening, watching, making it a point to be everybody's friend. There had been leads, some worthless, some hopeful. Twice she had left town to track down clues, to try to find men who knew. Futilely. The wave of violence had risen higher and higher in Bridger despite Adam Blair, the new sheriff, despite the secret Vigilantes.

"Once, a man in his cups – orey-eyed – babbled the name of John Hugo. It seems he was a small-town lawman who'd traced a man here . . . that John Hugo knew something – and had not sunk from sight as had so

155

many others. The man said he was down in Crosby, told me the name of a girl who knew John Hugo. I went to Crosby, won the confidence of this girl. But John Hugo had been swallowed too . . . If you learn anything in Bridger – I know now – you just – just disappear." She shuddered.

Dornan rose to put some fresh wood in the stove. A shadow had fallen over Red's lean features. Hugo, the name reminded him of his lost brother, Hugo Paine. Charlie, dead . . . He himself, a lobo . . . Hugo, Lord knew where. It seemed a pitiful payoff for all that Big Red his father had struggled to do, for the high hopes he'd had for his boys.

"Last spring, I came back here and taught school, hoping . . . hoping . . ." There had been rumors. Leads, again. Once, the father of a pupil, near the close of the school term, had come and begged her to take his young son away with her when she went home. He'd offered her plenty of dinero to take care of the boy. "Two nights later he was found dead."

And then, one evening, she had stumbled over a poor devil on a side street, knifed and dying. With his final breath he'd told her to look up a man named Dick the Gambler. This Dick was a fool over women and might tell things to one who worked on him right. Dick the Gambler, the dying man said, then

156

worked as a house guard in a dancehall in Encinto. She'd gone there and gotten a job. That was where Red had last encountered her.

"I played up to Dick the Gambler," she related with hard eyes. Evidently it had been a distasteful job. He'd begun to talk a little. It seemed her father was but one of many whose families now paid ransom for a man they knew was still alive but would never see again. And Dick had laughed about the Law, even U.S. marshals if they should be sent in, never doing anything about breaking the black terror that held Bridger in its clutch. He said tough John Laws had come in on the trail of pards who'd vanished, then ridden out as meek as sheep.

Doc looked up from the quirly he built and cut his eyes at Red as if to say, "What did I tell you?"

Dick the Gambler had begun to drop names. And then, once, holding her in his arms, believing he had made a new conquest, he'd mentioned a man known simply as "Joe." Said this Joe knew a heap, was free, and was totally unsuspected by the power that actually ruled Bridger. That very evening, Dick the Gambler had been shot dead as he left his boarding house in Encinto to go on duty.

"This time I realized I was marked myself," Peg Dana said slowly. "So I came back here disguised as a man. I found Joe. He's known here and in Crosby as Loco Joe. Folks think he's a harmless fool ... He isn't. He plays that role to stay alive ... I've gotten him to the point of trusting me. The last time, he admitted he knew some things – not everything. He was going to say more. Then – well, did you notice the blond bartender at that place where you saved me?"

The trio nodded quickly. They had all right.

"Well, a man just like him – it must have been his brother – got Loco Joe and they rode off together."

Red, Doc and Bill Dornan exchanged glances.

"Joe sent me word – up here. So he must have been all right. I was to meet him today down there. Then – *they* –" She paused. "Now, they'll kill Loco Joe, silence another one, I suppose ... "

CHAPTER SIXTEEN

Again the three men exchanged glances. Doc said to Peg:

"The brother of the blond bartender – he's the one we are after, miss. Ed Rader."

She nodded. It didn't mean much to her then. Dornan asked permission, then lighted up his cigar stub. He paced around, saw one of his shirt tails was loose and colored furiously. He said:

"That fits right in about Ed being in this game here ... One night when he was lickered up and bragging a heap, he told me he'd worked with a really big bunch before throwing in with us. And that he'd had to get out for a while because he got mixed up with a skirt – pardon me, ma'am – a woman who belonged to another of the outfit. But he said when things cooled off he figured to go back with 'em ... Looks like he has."

She took a box of matches off a shelf as Red, with a fresh smoke in his mouth, couldn't find one in his pockets. She seemed terribly weary. It was discouragement.

"I had such high hopes when I rode down into town today. Joe was to meet me there this

evening. I knew I'd learn a lot more. Yet I –
I had a premonition of trouble. I stopped in
Sheriff Blair's office and spoke to him."

Doc shook his head. " 'S Foolish to tell
the Law anything, ma'am. Tin badgers like
to boast. They spread it around, what they
know. Then *everybody* knows it."

Peg said, "I didn't tell him anything,
really. I'd noticed lately two different men
at different times – but always the same ones
– following me when I was in town. I told the
sheriff I might be on the verge of finding out
something about these killings in Bridger."

"Yes?" snapped Red so that she looked up
quickly.

"Well, nothing. Mr. Blair seemed very
interested. He was very nice. I described
the two men to him so that in case anything
happened to me, they'd know where to look.
Then, later in the day, a strange man stepped
up to me in a store and said I was wanted
down there at that barroom. He left before
I could ask any questions. I knew Loco Joe
was due in. So I went down there – and
then . . ."

There was no need to say any more, and
there was little they could say to her. It
seemed a hopeless game she was bucking.
She'd been twisting at a shirt button
nervously. It came off. Womanlike, she

160

went into the back room of the cabin to get a needle and thread. The three men stood by the open front door, looking out at the rain-washed world, as the afternoon neared its close. Then Red Paine spoke.

"Doc – Bill – I'm not walking out on you gents. But –" He halted. This girl, Peg Dana, had saved his hide twice. And even if she had done nothing for him, he couldn't have walked out to let her shift for herself in her gallant single-handed gamble against the evil thing in Bridger. Perhaps it was the "wild fool blood" in him, as his dad had once described the crazy streak in the Paines. Red cleared his throat.

Dornan hitched at his pants. "I was in love once with a copper-haired girl . . . They got spitfire tempers, though, Red."

"Shut up," Red grated. "Look. I – I got to try to help, 's all. Maybe I can't do much. This is tough. But –"

"Three of us can do more," Doc said.

Red stared at them, started to speak. Bill Dornan said, "Shut up. Your paw was a fine man, but he never taught you when to keep your big mouth shut. Shucks, we'd be behind bars now if you hadn't pulled that trick at Donnelville."

"But I can't ask you fellas –"

"You ain't," Doc said, spitting out the door

161

into the grass. "We're *telling* you, button. 'Sides, Rader seems mixed up in this game anyway. So deal us cards while you're so busy cutting yourself in too."

"This Loco Joe, he seems like the key . . . unless they silence him too."

"Wait. . . ." Red was thinking. He turned as Peg Dana re-entered the room. "Peg – I mean – Miss Dana, if you aren't there to meet this Loco Joe when he comes in, what happens then?"

"Why –" Her hand went to her lips. "Why, he'll come here. He said he'd be there sometime this afternoon. He'll come here and –" She didn't want to say it. She swallowed hard.

Red rubbed the palms of his hands hard on his tied-down holsters. "He'll come here – and lead them to you. . . ."

Back in the town as the last rays of the sun slanted over the jagged peaks in the west, Red and Doc, hats low, strayed around the main drag above the side road that led down to the little bar where they'd found Peg. Doc, taking a long-shot chance, had already worked up the side road from the other end, slipped into the empty lot, and taken a looksee at the place. There had been no gent answering Loco Joe's description there, no big towering ponderous-bodied fellow with great sad eyes

162

flanking a prodigious hook of nose. Now they were hanging around to intercept him when and if he did come.

It was Saturday and the range town was packed with everybody in to do their marketing, many of the men preparing for their Saturday night blowout. Down the road a little, on the steps of a honky tonk, a frock-coated man waved a fistful of pink tickets and bawled over and over that this was the night of the big raffle at the place. Buck boards, wagons, buggies, rigs of all kinds as well as a steady procession of riders splashed through the puddles and black mud of the broad road. Throngs jostled each other in a slow procession on the wooden sidewalks. Across the road, a travelling dentist had set up a tent between two stores and was doing a rushing business.

In all that hubbub and excitement, Red and Doc Sills felt fairly safe from recognition. Then, suddenly, the crowd on the walk on that side began to split in an avenue. A stocky man in a pinch-topped black sombrero with a flat brim, tailed by two taller men, came striding along rapidly.

"Here comes Sheriff Blair," said somebody near Red and Doc. It was too late to get away. Doc shifted quickly as they pressed against the front of a barbershop,

163

turning his big back toward the approaching law boss of Bridger so as to screen Red. He told him to keep his head bent as if about to light the fresh quirly in his mouth when Adam Blair passed. . . .

Red felt his hands twitch to fold around the ivory gun butts, grimly fought off the impulse. It seemed as if every nerve in his trigger fingers shrieked for action. The blood was sucked from his face. But he ruled himself with that iron will, edged his head slightly to see beyond Doc Sill's high-set shoulder. It was an incredible thing, he realized. This man approaching had led the posse that had burnt down his father for something he'd never done. This man approaching he hated with a terrible hate, a hate held in leash only because his dad wanted it that way. Yet, Red, had never clapped eyes on the gent before.

He saw him. Blair was all in black. And there was something almost Napoleonic about him as he strode on short legs with a slight stoop that belittled his stature. Hands clasped behind him, black coat flapping over the double-holstered gunbelt, boot heels snapping on the boards, he came down the line. His chin was pressed down on his white shirt and black bow tie. Looking neither to right nor left, he greeted nobody. There was a broad-jawed face, a sharp-tipped nose, eyebrows like black bars. He looked implacable, coldly merciless, the breed to be swerved by nothing, by no man. The two taller deputies followed him like shadows, matching steps with his though they were longlegged.

"Easy, kid, easy," Doc Sills whispered.

For Red Paine stood a-quiver like a half-tamed horse feeling the bridle bit for the first time. A bead of perspiration threaded its way down the side of his face, looping over bunched jaw muscles. His nostrils were wide-flaring as he sucked in wind. And the gray eyes had an almost unholy glitter while the measured rap of those boot heels played a tattoo on his very heart.

Doc grabbed Red's hat brim to make him look down as Adam Blair drew abreast. Doc knew the whole story of Red's dad. One night in the camp in the hills Red had related it. Then, without warning, Adam Blair turned sharply, grunted at a child in his way, and crossed the street. The crowd swirled in behind him. Red tried to put the match to his cigarette, but his hands trembled like a palsied man's. Doc had to do it for him. Red knew then the truth of another thing his dad used to say. That to keep yourself in rein when you wanted to stampede wildly was one of the hardest things a man could do. For some moments, he actually felt sick.

More and more lights went on along the road. Music came from one of the honky tonks. Dusk closed in. They edged down the grade of the side street and saw the bar boss, Ed Rader's brother, standing on a chair as he lighted the lamp inside the place.

Half an hour later, with Bridger swinging into the full swing of its wanton night life, Red said, "Reckon he won't be coming." They agreed to pull out. With darkness fallen, he could slip in without their spotting him. After all, actually, they didn't know him.

They picked up the girl's claybank pony at the hitchrail on the main line where she had left it before entering the barroom earlier that day, were just moving toward their own horses, walking along the gutter. Then a tall gent stepped out from the throng, stared at Red. It was the one he had deputed to keep the crowd out of that side road when he'd posed as a law officer earlier that day.

"That's him! That's the gent who was in that barroom shooting down there!" the tall man began to scream, stepping back but levering a long arm at Red Paine.

"You're orey-eyed again, you old fool!" Red yelled back as he and Doc moved along faster. But men were turning, picking them out.

"It's him, I tell you! He's the one —"

166

Doc swore under his breath. They were still some distance from where they'd left their own ponies. And then two galloping riders came bursting into that end of the main road from the trail westward. They reined up, splashing mud wildly as the horses sought to block their hoofs in the mud. One of them yelled for the sheriff.

"The stage coming down with the gold shipment from the Staghorn Mine," he pointed toward the peaks up to the northwest, "she was robbed *again!*" he bawled. "Bad, too. Three men killed! And they had a double guard along with her too, eight of 'em. It was a special run of the stage. It was supposed to be a secret when she was coming down! And –"

"But *they* knew all right," cut in the quieter rider. "Where's Blair?"

A man in stovepipe hat beside Red shook his head ruefully. "That's the third time in five weeks they've jumped the stage coming in from the mine. . . . This country has turned bad clean through!"

Overflowing from the sidewalk, gathering like flies, thick-pressed, the crowd filled the road, hungry for more information. The shouting of the tall jasper who'd recognized Red Paine was drowned out, forgotten. Then a lanky man with long black mustaches and a gray frock coat leaped onto the edge of

167

a watering trough and began to rant at the crowd. He said he'd be the first to volunteer to ride into the hills and stick there till they found those devils. He said everybody had to back the Law.

"Robles," said the man in the stovepipe hat. "A regular fire-breather, too. He's head of the Vigilantes, the only member known."

Pushing and half circling, Red and Doc cut out of the mob and got down to their own ponies. A man watching from the doorway said:

"They'll be a stop to this now that Tentrus is back!"

Red whistled softly. He hadn't realized the full risk he'd taken in returning to Bridger City again this day. . . .

CHAPTER SEVENTEEN

Back up at the cabin, Peg Dana tried to tell them again they ought to pull stakes. Red gave her a mischievous wink.

"We like it here," he said.

They were simply deaf to the rest of her arguments, even tried to hide their worry. But they all knew what could happen. Loco

Joe might get into town later and, failing to find her, come up to the cabin. And there was the danger, almost a probability if he returned, that he would be trailed. Unwittingly he would lead the mysterious "them" to her.

The girl already had dinner cooking on the stove. Bill Dornan sniffed the aroma of it hungrily, pushed in his shirt, picked up the carbine from his saddle boot. "I'll just mosey down the line a little," he said.

Red and Doc understood. Dornan would stand guard for a spell.

Despite the tension, the threat hanging over them, it was the finest meal Red Paine had eaten for years. Afterward as they sat smoking, a dreamy light came into his habitually guarded eyes. Sitting over a table after some well-cooked chow like that, in a homelike atmosphere, with a pretty girl opposite him, was something completely new to him. And it opened unsuspected vistas. Made him ponder on what it might be like to be settled down with a home of his own, a wife, knowing where he would be laying his head each night. Then he throttled his imagination brutally. That could never be for him. He was a pariah, a man marked from birth. He would always be on the run, never knowing when he would be a hunted thing, never knowing where he would roll into his blanket.

"Well, I'll go down and relieve Bill, Red. You can help Miss Peg do the dishes, I reckon," Doc said with a saccharine smile as he pushed back his chair.

Peg Dana was already smiling shyly. But Red thrust up so sharply he almost upset the table. "I'll take Bill's place," he bit off brusquely, snatching up his hat and marched out.

He didn't come back from down by the bend of the path till he saw the lamp go out in the cabin's second room, meaning the girl had turned in. He and Doc and Dornan held a conference there before the cabin with the gentle swish of the trees overhead. Doc cocked a weather eye and predicted there'd be a moon a little after midnight. They decided to take turns standing guard right through the night. It didn't look as if Loco Joe had turned up. But they couldn't afford to take any risks.

Red took the first shift, sitting on a rock back from the path to the cabin at the bend a little below the shelf where it stood. He forced his mind away from any thoughts concerning the copper-haired girl. With his kind of life, there was nothing he could offer a woman. He recalled the picture of the stocky, implacable-faced man who had come down the sidewalk that afternoon. Adam Blair. It was strange the role the man had played in his life, how it had warped all of it. And still, if this Loco Joe should come, if he could give Peg some real information as he'd hinted, they might have to turn to Blair for aid in breaking this lawless dynasty that ruled Bridger City.

The hours seeped away slowly. Once a couple of gunshots floated up faintly from the main road down near Bridger. Aside from that, all was still. A coyote bayed in the distance for a while. And there was the constant lulling murmur of the treetops in the wind. Then Doc came down the path to relieve him. They talked a few moments. Red went up to the cabin, pulled off his boots, and stretched on the floor beside the snoring Bill Dornan. Though he could neither see nor hear her, the outlaw's son was acutely aware of the girl sleeping in the next room. She would make such a fine partner to go through life with for a man who didn't bear the stigma he did. If he hadn't been branded as the double-crossing deputy of Red Hat he might have considered asking her. . . .

There was no need for Bill Dornan, who'd taken the third guard shift of the night, to warn them. The rifle shot punched a clean sharp hole in the dawn. Right atop it came two fainter short gun cracks like weaker echoes. Ramming their feet into their boots, the slim Red and big Doc came piling out of the cabin. This was it, they knew.

Strapping on gunbelts, they hustled down to where Bill Dornan was posted. He was the epitome of calmness, picking his teeth with a homemade toothpick as he peered through the foggy air down the path.

"Visitors a-coming, I reckon," he noted casually.

The day was just breaking. Up there in the timber there was a hush without a leaf stirring as if in honor of its birth. When a bird called once it was like a harsh scratch on the surface of that serenity. From the distance, after another minute, they heard the quick rattle of horse hoofs over a rocky spot.

"Get the girl," Doc said.

Red was already hurrying back to the cabin. Before he got there, she stepped out the door in her jeans, a man's coat over her shirt, wearing her sombrero. And about her hour-glass waist was a gunbelt with a pearl-handled .32 slung in the holster. Red felt a gush of relief. No ordinary simpering female of a woman this. She'd had the sense

172

to sleep with her clothes on so she'd be ready.

"We won't have time for breakfast, I guess," she said calmly.

They moved back down the path together. It was still again, an ominous tense quiet. Red wanted to scout on down the hill to see what was going on. Doc slapped him roughly on the back.

"Don't try to be no danged hero," he told him. "Let them ride into us. They won't be expecting a greeting. And you take care of Miss Peg when the welcoming committee opens proceedings." They talked a little more, discussing plans. There was another gunshot reverberating amongst the hills, closer this time.

Dornan carefully tucked in his shirt, picked up his carbine and crossed the path to work into the undergrowth there. Came the sharp quick cry of a hurt man. From further down there was some yelling. The drum of hoofs on the soft ground got nearer. Then, it couldn't have been more than a few hundred feet off, there was the gasping of a struggling man. Gun hammers cocked. Trigger fingers crooked.

"Loco Joe," called the girl guardedly, and she was pointing down to a thicket to one side of the big dead pine.

Crouched like an animal, a huge hulking

figure of a man, staring back over his shoulder a moment, pushed into sight from the foliage. They could see the blood on the side of his head, and another stain on the left side of his hickory shirt that was almost black-soaked with sweat as it was. He wavered in his tracks, badly hurt, hesitated. He looked at the Colts he held. Then he slung it away because it was empty, disappeared behind a chunk of rock a moment. When he came into sight again he was running hard as if in drunken zigzags up the hill, bulling through underbrush, heading for the cabin. The eyes beside his huge hook of nose bulged with the tremendous effort he was making.

From down an avenue in the timber, an unseen rifleman cut down on him. Bullets slashed the leaves around him, gouged bark from a tree he had rested against a moment before. He threw himself in one tremendous bound and reached the path and came churning his way up it. Then he began to weave and wobble and stray from right to left like an animal suddenly gone blind.

Big Doc, still in his undershirt, jumped out and grabbed at him. "I'm with Miss Peg," he cried. It was all he needed to say. Loco Joe, head rocking on his powerful shoulders, knees buckling, allowed himself to be led. Doc signalled for Red to come up.

They got Joe off the path as a rifle slug grooved the packed earth of it ten yards down.

Red Paine knew better than to take Joe to the cabin. That could be a trap. That would be the target the bunch coming up the hill would drive for. He drew him back into the woods and Peg came up and spoke to Joe. The big man pawed at the blood on the side of his face and grinned faintly.

"I need a drink bad," he mumbled. "Tell the barkeep I – I –" He almost collapsed then. No longer did he even know where he was.

Red gave her a sign and Peg helped the big brute deeper in amongst the trees. There was a yell so close by it sounded on top of them. The smash of pony hoofs. Then brush was crashing all round. Doc turned and gestured Red to retreat.

"Stay back far enough!" he cried.

The first masked horseman appeared suddenly at the hump on the path some fifty-sixty feet down. Two more pushed into view through the heavy foliage some distance to the right of the path. Dornan's guns cut loose with a staccato bass chatter. One saddle was empty. Roaring with gusto, Doc hit the trigger and chimed in with him. The woods seemed to sprout charging riders who'd spread

175

out in a fan as they drove upward to try to capture Loco Joe.

Red barked at the girl to get Joe deeper into the woods. Bent behind a stump, he sent two stabs of gunfire toward the men driving in, saw one twist in sharp pain in the saddle. They were all masked with neckerchiefs. Two of them had dismounted and were trying to slip up the path on foot. Then Red and the girl were almost cut off. He heard the smash as a slug caromed off a boulder behind him. Whipping about, he saw the rider charging in from far to the right of the path.

It was the poised Peg's shot that brought him up sawing on the reins with a slug in one arm. Red darted down toward him a few steps and hit the trigger. The man slowly went up rigid in the saddle. Daylight showed between it and his pants a moment as he hung suspended. And then he plunged off, dead even as he dived in the undergrowth.

Red retreated still more, much as he hated to. But there was the girl to be shielded. Plus that, she had Loco Joe in tow. And he could be the most important of them all, holding, as perhaps he did, the key to the whole thing.

The crackle of fire dropped a moment. Then it burst afresh with renewed life like a swarm of bees landing. A slug from

176

somewhere just nicked the brim of Red's sombrero. Up there by the path, big Doc reared into sight, hands starting up as a man afoot with levelled smoke-wreathed gun closed on him. Red gave a soundless cry and rushed forward. There was no need. The next instant, with a sort of careless gesture, Doc had "Molly," his club, out of his belt behind his left hip, swishing forward. The gunman folded up in a patch of grass. Doc calmly picked up his Colts and began to thumb fresh cartridges into them.

The fight began to peter out. "They," the masked riders, had expected no such reception. Red looked back. He couldn't see Peg, who'd been half dragging Loco Joe back. Red darted back in the direction she'd been moving, fear like a grisly finger hooking into his heart. There was a small ledge of outcropping rock. He hurled himself around the edge of it and the cold dread fell away from him. Back beyond the little ledge was a small clearing. The girl was crouched back in the grass at one edge of it, her .32 drawn. And Red knew Loco Joe must be stretched prone somewhere near her.

Moving back toward the path, he sighted one horseman plunging down the hill pell mell. There was a last shot. Then the crash of the underbrush as more riders dragged their tails out of there. Bill Dornan waved from between the trees further over. There was some blood on his shirt sleeve from a nick in the arm. For once, he was actually grinning.

"They never said goodbye," he called.

Everything was all right. They had Joe. Red turned and headed back to where Peg had dragged him. He went around the other end of the ledge that time and approached the clearing from the upper side. Through the leaves, he glimpsed Peg Dana standing, gun pointed, facing his way. Cocking both hammers, the outlaw's son slipped forward. He moved around the bole of a huge tree. Ten feet ahead, on the fringe of that side of the clearing, stood a huge rangy-shouldered figure. The left hand hanging by the man's side had the first two fingers missing.

Jud Tentrus! And he had himself under control. No son of Big Red Paine's would ever shoot a man in the back.

"Mis-ter Tentrus, I believe," Red said dryly.

Tentrus started to spin. Red's shot deliberately went through the crown of the manhunter's sombrero harmlessly. And Tentrus, no fool, knowing when the trap was sprung, flung up his arms, his gun dropping into the grass.

178

CHAPTER EIGHTEEN

When he turned completely, Tentrus recognized the advancing Red Paine at once. The lawman's hardbitten red face, despite his imminent danger, framed itself into a sneer.

"A bad penny always turns up, like they say, eh," he said calmly. "I might've known when I sloped back into this devil's town it'd be the kind of a place where you'd thrive! Bad blood always —"

Red trembled as he advanced on him. All the things, all the references Tentrus had made once before to his parentage flooded back into his head. It was hard not to kill this man in his tracks. "If you want to keep yours inside your skin, a spell, don't talk about blood," Red warned.

Tentrus breathed hard, loudly. He said, "So you're one of those masked snakes I followed up —"

Red dug his Colts muzzle into Tentrus' belly so that the big man had to break off as the wind was knocked from him. Red called him a fool and said he'd been fighting those masked sidewinders. "But you came with them, Tentrus! Maybe you can explain that to Blair the sheriff?"

"Came with them? Me?" Tentrus frowned as he tried to understand. His belligerence eased a moment. He said he'd been up all night, scouting around Bridger. Just as daylight broke, he'd seen these riders out on the trail and had taken after them. In the hills, he had lost them for a spell. And when the firing led him to the spot, he had circled around to try to find out what the game was.

The two mutually hating men locked glances. And in that instant, they had one thing in common. Each knew the other was not lying. Red nodded, then ran over Tentrus for a hideout weapon, found a smaller gun in a special armpit holster, threw it into the grass.

There was a call, Dornan and Doc moved into the clearing, half carrying a wounded man between them. The latter had been hit in the leg and had a bullet hole between his ribs. His neckerchief mask had slipped back down around his neck. Red stared at the gent. It was the lanky man with the long black mustaches who'd climbed up on the horse trough and harangued the crowd about law and order down in Bridger last evening when the news had come in about the stage holdup. The man the gent in the stovepipe hat had identified as Robles, head man of the Vigilantes. Tentrus, recognizing him too, let out a roar, cursing a blue streak.

"Robles, you dirty snivelling double-crossing rat!" the lawman boomed. "Why –" Then he remembered the girl standing a few yards away and broke off to apologize. As if he were no prisoner himself, Tentrus walked up to Robles, seized his face by the chin. He fired questions at him. Robles, weak from loss of blood and half out on his feet, only stared at the ground sullenly, refusing to answer. Tentrus started to cuff him around. But the girl cried out and he stopped.

"We'll find out a few things when we git you down to the jailhouse, anyway!" Tentrus promised.

"Who said you're going back?" Bill Dornan asked him, recognizing the famed manhunter.

Over in the grass, Loco Joe moaned and threshed around a little. Peg said he was in a bad way. Red and Doc and Dornan conferred a few moments. There would be no danger for a while. The masked riders had left three dead out there in the woods. They'd be licking their wounds for some little time. The three decided to go back to the cabin.

Back there, the silent Robles' leg was tied up to stop the bleeding. But Loco Joe was the one they really worked over, Peg and

Doc together. Dornan told them something while they did.

"Reckon we won't ever be able to settle the way we wanted with Ed Rader," he said to Doc and to Red, who carefully kept Tentrus covered every instant. The latter seemed in a daze himself. He couldn't understand the setup.

"Why?" asked Doc, looking up. They'd staunched the wound in poor Loco Joe's side. The head wound was nasty, but the slug had gone clear through the flesh. And while the skull might have been creased, it was not punctured. The big sad-eyed man was half conscious, even mumbling at times, but out of his mind temporarily.

"Well," and Dornan looked very sheepish about it, "a fella jumps outa the brush right in the middle of that melee. He didn't know I was so close. I let him have it smack through the chest, dead center. He was shaking hands with the angels afore he hit the ground. Then – well, then his mask slipped off. . . . Fellas, it was Ed Rader. And he died too plumb easy. I – I'm right danged sorry."

There was a brief struggle as Loco Joe tried to fight his way out of the chair they'd propped him in. Then Peg spoke to him softly and he relaxed. "Tell the barkeep if he don't bring me that drink pronto, I'm goin to change his face," he muttered.

Tentrus asked permission to light up a quirly. Red gave him a nod. The towering lawman pulled a tailor-made quirly from his pocket and fired it up. The harsh self-assured air was gone from him now. "Paine, what kind of a hand are you dealing here?" he asked. The habitual note of command was missing from his voice.

"Trying to break this thing that rules Bridger City – whatever the thing is," Red said a little wearily.

"What?" barked Tentrus.

"But that is unimportant right now. You and I have an old score to settle." It was hard to hold himself in. The eyes of the girl and his two saddle pards were locked on him.

Tentrus drew himself up; he packed nerve. "Give me my cutter back – and I'll settle it with you, Paine!"

It was a terrible temptation. Outside, the rays of the risen sun dappled the grass before the cabin with golden splotches. A soft breeze stirred the trees. Through the doorway, down in the direction of the town, light bluish smoke sailed in a slow spiral from the chimney of an unseen house. Red Paine looked out at those things. This man, Tentrus, he hated almost as bitterly as he did Blair. Red spoke very very slowly.

"You gave me no weapon to defend myself with that night in the jailhouse, Tentrus. . . . No. . . ." He lifted his Colts muzzle to bear on the man. "Now – maybe you'd like to get down on your knees and beg for your life. Yes?"

Peg Dana started to move from the room. She made no protest. She had been there that night in the jailhouse. And she understood this was a thing two men had to settle, that there was no alternative.

"Wait." Red made a motion with his head for her to stay.

Sweat stood out like a glassy little mustache on Jud Tentrus' upper lip. He put his cigarette to his mouth, drew deep, then tossed it through the doorway. He nodded. "Trigger when you're ready, Paine. I go on my knees for no man, by Gawd!"

"Step outside," Red said softly.

The four men moved out into the open space before the cabin, Doc making certain Robles was securely trussed first. The Vigilante boss who'd apparently gone bad sat glassy-eyed, stunned, as if he no longer understood what went on around him. Outside, Red kept nervously flipping the gun he ached to loose in the road agent's spin. He was fighting for control every instant. Thinking of his dad. Swallowing and re-swallowing his hate for this law hound, and still the hate kept bubbling up into his throat again. His dad had told him many a time that a man had to be big no matter what happened. And Harry Westfall used to keep telling him so often he had to be different from others.

This, he knew, was the greatest test he had faced. He had to force back personal enmity. Later there might come a time when he could settle with Tentrus. But now, Tentrus could be valuable to them. Red said:

"Tentrus, I could give you your gun – and still kill you almost as easily as I can now with you unarmed."

Tentrus started to guffaw. Something about the terrible solemnity of Red Paine's face broke it off short. Red pointed down to a tree some fifteen paces away.

"See that white patch?" he asked. It was where the bark had been ripped and a small splotch of fungus growth had attached itself.

Tentrus nodded. Red holstered his gun. He plucked a cartridge from his gunbelt. He stretched out his right arm stiffly, parallel to the ground. He put the shell on the top of his flattened hand.

"Watch how death would hit you, Tentrus." A moment passed. Then the cartridge was falling through empty air. Red's hand flashed down with that incredible speed that was his heritage, the heritage of a man born to the gun. Before they could see the hand touch holster, the Colts was out, spitting jagged powderflame from its ugly muzzle. Two little black marks appeared in the fungus growth down there, bullet holes. And the fallen cartridge, dropped from the back of Red's hand, was just rolling away from the small half-buried stone it had hit with a slight *ping*.

Tentrus stood with his jaw sagging open so that two gold-capped teeth in the back of his head showed. Red Paine was like a stick of wood.

"No accident – again," he said quietly.

He put a second shell on the back of his hand. There was a second in which everything seemed to stand still. Then the blurred flash of the hand down to the gun scabbard. The gleaming Colts barrel like a live thing leaping into the air, horizontal, seeming a part of Red Paine's hand. The double crash of the two reports almost like one. Drifting gunsmoke blurred their vision a moment. And then they saw the two fresh black marks like dull nailheads in the fungus on the tree trunk.

"You see how I could do it – kill you?" Red asked.

Tentrus stood staring at the slim man with

186

the now dead gray eyes. And though he was helpless, probably due to get his light put out in one way or another, the famed law hound's face glowed with admiration.

"I never seen shooting like that in my life," he said.

Red let out his breath like a man coming up from under water after a long spell. He had gone through something terrible. He felt a full year more mature. This decision he had arrived at had cost him something.

Walking over, he picked up Tentrus' two guns where he'd dropped them beside the cabin door when they came in. He came back and handed them to Jud Tentrus.

"All right. Now you know I could kill you if I so willed," Red said, his voice suddenly hoarse with the strain. "Now take your prisoner, Robles, into the sheriff, Tentrus. Some other day . . . you and I . . ."

CHAPTER NINETEEN

The other three men could not believe it at first. Tentrus even dropped one of the guns handed him. Doc's eyebrows climbed halfway to the bald fore part of his head. Dornan

187

choked, then expostulated:

"Red, are you locoed? Why this danged –"

Red's eyes switched to him and Dornan stopped talking.

Tentrus spat dryly into the grass. He looked at Red again. "This – this – it's some trick," he said.

Red scourged him with a look. "Do *I* need tricks?"

Tentrus shook his head slowly. "I don' understand."

It was Red who was sweating now "Tentrus, this time we're both on the sam side. We want to smash this black evil that' poisoned this piece of country." He nodded toward the cabin and told Tentrus quickl about Peg Dana's father who'd vanishe here but who they knew still lived. He wa unaware the girl was just inside a window hearing it all, and that her eyes were mist with pure admiration for the magnificence o this slim man who'd had the score against hin all his life.

"We want the same thing, Tentrus," Re finished. "We can work together – till th job is done. You're in there in town, on th inside. We have this Joe here. Perhaps h can give us something that will help us cu the sign of these snakes ... Together, mayb we can get them. Take in Robles. The les you tell Blair about us, probably, the better. That's all."

Tentrus wiped his mouth slowly. "How do I know you're dealing them straight?" he demanded, the old lawman strain coming to the fore.

Red sneered faintly, nodded down to the bullet-scarred tree. "You have to ask that, now?"

Tentrus seemed to collapse inside himself. Shame painted his big face with scarlet. In that moment, though he was half the lawman's size, Red Paine actually looked physically larger. He was the bigger man, inside if not in stature. Tentrus muttered something like an apology.

"All right," he said firmly. "We play out the string together!" He put out his hand.

Red Paine shook his head at it, refusing to shake. "No. . . . We just play it together!"

They moved, Dornan still grumbling that Red had been a danged fool. He said there was always the chance that Tentrus, who had outlaw-hate in his very veins, would bring out a bunch from town and grab them.

But they left the cabin, the girl, the outlaw trio, and Loco Joe. They had lifted him into the saddle of Red's Cayuse. And again he and Peg Dana rode double, both of them on her pony. It was on Tentrus' advice that they

189

did clear out. He warned them there was no telling when the masked gents would return with fresh men. He'd mentioned the old Proctor place down on the main trail several miles to the west of the town. Proctor had been killed a few weeks ago and the place was empty. The very fact that it was in the open, smack on the road, would make it the last place anybody would look for them so long as they kept out of sight. And Peg Dana had echoed his advice.

So they crossed over through the broken country, worked down out of the hills warily. Doc had to ride with one big arm thrust about Joe to keep the latter in the saddle. Loco Joe was still out of his mind. They dropped into a little swale. Then they moved up through a clump of cottonwoods to the ramshackle two-story place after a couple of riders had gone from sight out on the road. And the long vigil began.

They put Joe on a bunk built into one of the rooms and waited. Peg nursed him carefully, applying wet cloths to his feverish head, working a little of the whisky Doc produced between his lips at intervals. But Joe tossed. Sometimes he talked. He kept calling for the bar boss to bring that drink. Once he got to mumbling about his mother. Red mentioned bringing out a pill roller

But it was the girl who shook her head. No move was made in Bridger that "they" didn't know about. To bring a doctor here would be as good as signing Loco Joe's death warrant. And they didn't argue because they realized she knew conditions far better than they did. They ate some of the cold grub they'd brought down from the cabin, gulped water from the well after it. They didn't dare even make hot coffee. Smoke from the stove chimney of the deserted place might have attracted attention. The day dragged away, the evening stage from the west rattled by with two extra guards riding behind it as the last ray of sunlight spiked around one of the jagged peaks.

Doc tried to entertain them with yarns about his old Bible-pounding days, but he soon gave it up. They were all on pins and needles. Talk was meaningless and simply irritating. Their one big hope, their lone hole card, lay in there on the bunk, babbling now about fishing in some creek when he was a boy in Montana.

They slept little during the night, catnapping off and on, one of them always watching the road. Once Red went in to relieve the girl sitting beside Loco Joe. He really seemed locoed then as he muttered over and over again, "It's awful ... plumb

awful what they – they do in the Castle.'
He sounded like somebody quoting from a
fairy tale.

Peg went out and rested in an old chair in
the front room for a spell. Dark circles already
ringed her eyes. But inside an hour, she was
back, refusing to rest more. They whispered
beside the bunk. Red was beginning to lose
hope, he admitted.

But Peg shook her head. "I don't know
– but something tells me he wouldn't have
fought through to my cabin unless he had
something terribly important to tell me . .
He must have known *they* had discovered he
was betraying them. They'd evidently shot
his horse from under him. . . . But up there
in the timber he would have had a chance of
escaping if he hadn't tried to keep coming up
the path."

Red hoped she was right. He found himself
getting a surge of anger at every mention of
the mysterious unknown "they."

"Hello, Mother," Joe said suddenly
clearer-voiced, and tried to sit up. "Ol'
Mother Johns! He-he. . . . Have a drink,
Mother. Straight from the bottle like always,
huh? Haw-haw." And he began to sing
brokenly snatches from a bawdy refrain.

Red looked up at Doc, who'd appeared in
the doorway in his stocking feet. They both

had the same thought. This Joe actually *was* locoed. Outside of any deliriousness, he was reliving scenes he'd experienced. And none of it made sense. Mother Johns – with his last name Alsop, as Peg had told them – could hardly be his mother. And you didn't talk about any mother taking drinks from a bottle.

Day came. And a little after sunrise, Jud Tentrus rode by on the road outside, whistling loudly to attract their attention. A little while later, he came up to the back of the house through the cottonwoods. He looked haggard and his eyes stared hard at some inanimate object when he talked to them inside. Red had the feeling that, under the circumstances, any other man would have been shifty-eyed.

"It's bad news, plumb bad news," he told the three men. "Robles never talked. Wouldn't say nothing. And – he won't, ever." He rubbed his chin, and Red noticed how he seemed to have aged in a matter of hours. "Robles was shot in his cell at the jail late last night."

It was a blow. If the head of the Vigilantes, who'd turned crooked, could have been made to talk, everything might have been cleared up. Tentrus gave them what bare details there were. Robles had been shot through the head, apparently as he stood at his cell window on the second floor, from the low

mound back beyond the yard of the jailhouse
He had been stone dead by the time Adam
Blair ran upstairs.

Red saw Peg Dana suck her lower lip in
saw her turn gray. Their chances seemed to b
running slimmer every hour. It was anothe
blow to this girl seeking to find her fathe
trapped in some living death.

Tentrus went back to town, seemingly
heavily discouraged himself. "I think he wa
holding back something," Dornan opined :
couple of times after the lawman left. Bu
there didn't seem much sense to that.

During that Monday that seemed to stretch
into eternity itself for those men forced int
inactivity, Loco Joe was very quiet in on hi
bunk. Then, late in the day, Red heard Pe
call. He hurried in. Joe was sitting up, eye
wide open, the vague insane light missing
from them momentarily.

"I know what – what it was now I wante
to tell – to tell," he said slowly, with th
obvious effort of a man straining to hol
his mind in line. "Sometime . . . sometim
early Tuesday, they're bringing a man to th
Castle. They usually bring them about daw
– or rather nightfall – to the Castle."

Red's hopes sagged again. The Castle. I
made no sense. It sounded like childis
prattle.

Loco Joe went on, his big hands knotted and twisted slowly as he dredged in his feverish mind. "Now, if you had friends . . . friends, you could bring a man to the Castle too. . . . Down there, they never know who might be bringing the man. The song – the song is –" He pawed feebly at his head. The password is a little song. "The song . . ." A humming sound came from his lips. He sang flatly, " 'I'll eat when I'm hungry . . . drink when – when I'm thirsty . . . and if whisky doesn't kill me . . . I – I'll live till I die.' "

He stopped. The blank stare returned to his eyeballs. Then the lids shuttered down. He lay back in the bunk.

"It doesn't make sense," said Dornan heavily in the door.

Red switched his eyes to Peg. He could see the unshed tears of bitter disappointment welling behind hers.

On the bed, Joe groaned. "Crosby, it's a terrible hole," he muttered. "Like – like a living graveyard. And the Castle." Then a scream ripped from him. "I know now," he yelled, flailing the blanket. "They're going to put me in the Castle too. *They* – they've found out I – I've been talking. I – I got to run." He started to kick. Then he sank into a stupor.

There was no warning of the final killing blow to their hopes, Peg didn't need to call that time. Red heard Joe say very clearly:

"Miss Peg, I came to tell you –"

All three men rushed in. From the sound of the voice, they knew Loco Joe had regained full consciousness, that he was in his right mind again. He was sitting up, feet on the floor, gripping the slight girl by the shoulders when they hurried in. They could see by his face that he was sane, out of the state of delirium.

"Miss Peg, I –" His great sitting frame jerked in a terrific convulsion. "I – they almost caught me. But I –" He clawed at his trouser. Then saliva ran in a slow stream from a corner of his mouth. His eyes sank inward. There was a weak rattling cough deep down in his throat.

Red pushed the girl aside. It wasn't right for a woman to look Death in the face. He took Joe's shoulders and eased him down. But even as the big sad-eyed man went flat he passed on. His face started to crinkle in a smile of pure peace. And then it froze. He was dead.

Peg Dana's dry sobs sounded from the front room as Red stood there in the light of the candle stub, staring down at the dead

196

man. He felt whipped himself, the insides sucked from him. The evening wind coughed dolefully around the old house. Something rattled faintly. Red looked down. Just by his boot toe, under the edge of the bunk, was a scrap of paper. He paid it no heed at first.

The candle flickered. The paper stirred, flipped over. There was writing on it. And then Red realized it was no faded old piece of paper that might have been left by the last tenant. The writing stood out clear and black. It could have fallen from the bunk. . . . from the pocket of the dead man. Red recalled how Joe had clawed at his trouser leg, near the pocket. Slowly he bent and picked it up, too embittered by smashed hopes to hope much now.

The first words leaped out of him, *"Miss Peg . . ."*

He didn't know it but he called to the others. Then he was over close to the fickle candlelight, reading it aloud. It was a note Joe had evidently written somewhere, in a great hurry, when he realized he might be caught. Red spoke the words quickly. It read:

Miss Peg . . . They're after me. Go to Crosby if you can get some friends to side you. Go to Redeye Jim's place. It is a bar. Do this very early on Tuesday morning. Have one of the

men go in. He is to ask for Mother Johns. He
is to tell her he is bringing a man from the boss
to the Castle. That is the only way you could
get into the Castle alive. The Castle is the
place where – Mother Johns can get you inside
the Castle safe. The password to Mother is . . .

There was a long silence in the room of death.
Dornan finally said, "That Castle stuff again.
It don't make sense."

Red never took his eyes from the paper,
reading and re-reading it, seeking to decode
it, to get the sense. He had a tight feeling in
his chest like a man clutching at a final straw
just before he sinks beneath the tide. "The
boss is sending – Did Joe ever say who the
boss was, Peg?"

She shook her head. "He didn't know that
himself."

Red reread the note once more, cut his eyes
to the dead man. Then the outlaw's son began
to laugh low and a little crazily. Doc began to
shake him.

"Wait – I savvy it," Red said. "Remember
how once when he was talking he said they
were bringing a man to the Castle every
Tuesday – tomorrow morning?" The other
nodded. "Well, that's it. In this note, he's
trying to tell Peg her only chance. That is to
get help and go out there to Crosby, posing as
198

men bringing in the – the prisoner, I guess. To go see this Mother Johns and tell her the boss sent them. Mother Johns can get you into the Castle safely. That's it. Joe figured out the only scheme. He –"

"But the password," Doc said gloomily. "His note ends there."

Red threw up his hand. "He gave the password in his delirium, that song – I remember it. I'll eat when I'm hungry ... drink when I'm thirsty ..."

CHAPTER TWENTY

" 'I'll eat when I'm hungry ... drink when I'm thirsty,' " Red Paine hummed under his breath. He'd been struck by a sudden dread of forgetting the words now he was almost on the threshold of the place where he would use them. For they were sitting in the trees on a little slope just over Crosby. The dawn was coming up. And they were about to make the grim gamble.

The three in their saddles – Red and Doc and Dornan – exchanged slow glances. They were none too sanguine. It wasn't for their own lives they feared so much, though, being

199

human, they preferred the state described as "quick" in the Bible. But the whole thing might prove an empty farce, something dreamed up by a disordered mind. There was the "Castle" referred to in Joe's note and in his ravings. It was the fantastic touch that made the whole thing unbelievable.

Red pinched out his quirly stub, tossed it away, pulled out his ivory-stocked hoglegs and checked them. When he had found the key to the thing, putting together the note and Joe's talk, last evening, they had made their decision. It was to come on to Crosby, just the three of them, and play it out. They'd almost had to hogtie Peg Dana to make her stay behind. And then they had come out, avoiding Bridger and cutting across country. Doc Sills knew this valley fairly well, having preached the gospel up and down it many years ago, before the railroad had come through. He'd brought them down to the edge of Crosby without touching the main trail from Bridger City.

The dawn turned rosier, the town below rising as if from some grayish sea. It lay in the bow of a shallow creek with bridges at both ends of its main road. It was a small town. But little straggling streets and alleys wriggled off down from one side of the business street toward the bow of the creek

That was Crosby's Whisky Row. And it was a big one for such a sized straggling pueblo out there on the edge of the badlands country. It was mute testimony to the fact that Crosby drew the scum overflow from Bridger.

Somebody said, "All right." They picked up their reins and rode out from the trees. The dawn tide rose higher. Doc rose up in his stirrups and pointed to the south, to the sere sandy flats out beyond the town. From their elevation they could see the big grayish blockpile shape out there.

"I remember that place," Doc said. "It was there when I came through here years back. Some crazy Irishman built it. Fella by the name of Riley. He had some fool idea about irrigating, bringing water in from the mountains over to the west. Said he was going to turn the flats into a Paradise and make it lush range for cows. And he was so locoed, he built that huge rancho first – before he died – called it – sure, Riley's Castle! He –"

They all reined up an instant. Riley's Castle. That could be the Castle Loco Joe had kept referring to. It was the first hopeful note. Red's jaw jutted. He nodded and they walked their ponies into the slumbering town. With the light heightening, they had no trouble finding Redeye Jim's place. For there was a sign attached to the blacksmith's barn on the business street, an arrow that pointed down one of the dim byways with "Redeye Jim's" lettered on it. They went down the elbowing lane between little close-huddled buildings.

There was one that had formerly been a house. Over the door, in the faint light, a lopsided sign proclaimed it "Redeye Jim's." They dismounted. Red began to hammer on the door. No window went up, above. But finally a dim voice called to ask what it was.

"We're from the boss," Red answered.

There was no sound for a while. Next, something like a creak inside the door. Another minute passed. From inside but from the back of the place, a voice said, "Come in." Red tried the knob. The door that had been barred before swung open.

Bright lamplight struck them in the face. They saw that the front part of the house had been converted into a barroom. It was still fetid with the odor of spilled whisky and old tobacco smoke. Red blinked against the light.

"Keep your dewclaws away from your guns," a man said.

Halfway up the stairs on one side, two hombres crouched with double-barrelled shotguns poking before them. Over on the other side, behind the bar counter, the head and shoulders of another gent appeared. He had them covered with a pair of sixes.

"What does the boss want?"

That voice was a woman's. And it came from straight ahead. She spoke again before Red could answer. "Close the door behind you, fool."

Doc did. Only then could they place her. She was at a partially opened door halfway back in the house, a big horse of a woman with snaky black hair straggling to her shoulders and paint-daubed face still filmy with sleep. But her buzzard eyes were wide awake.

"We're bringing a man out to the Castle as he sent you word," Red said as calmly as he could. This was the test, the crucial moment. And if it failed, they were right smack in the middle of a nice gun trap.

"Did he?" said the hoarse-voiced woman. "Never saw you before, young un. And speaking of words, do you know any?"

Red caught the cue. "Some," he came back. "And I sing real fine. Listen." He sang. " 'I'll eat when I'm hungry, drink when I'm thirsty, and if whisky doesn't kill me. I'll live till I die.' . . . How's that?"

There was a pause. It seemed half a lifetime to the trio.

Then the woman nodded, clutching the wrapper tighter about her. "It stinks. . . . But the words are good. I'll send the word to the Castle. Wait outside of town about ten minutes so's I can.... Then they'll let you in." The door through which she'd been speaking closed.

One of the men behind a shotgun on the stairs relaxed. "Hear they got a new bunch of girls at the dancehalls over in Bridger," he said.

Doc nodded. "Some pretty ones. Look me up if you come over."

They backed out the front door. Dornan sleeved the sweat from his face with a "Whew." It had been so simple. Of course what might happen at the Castle, what they would find there –

"Red!" Red Paine would have recognized that voice if he had heard a faint echo of it in the beyond. It was Peg. And then the crash of gunfire wiped it out for an instant. Bullets ripped into the front of the house around them. Their guns were still in their holsters. Doc jerked as he was nicked in the flesh of his upper right arm. They never had a chance.

Men darted out from the shadows, from up and down the alley, from between a couple of places across it. Two gun slicks edged around a corner of the house on whose steps they stood, covering them dead to rights.

"Surrender!" barked a voice that might have come from the iron-lined throat. "Hoist 'em!"

The cornered desperate Red Paine was about to make a play. Down the alley strode the stocky figure with the Napoleonic air, the sheriff of Bridger, Adam Blair himself. Red hesitated. And then it was too late. Striding to one side of him was a gunman. And that gunman had his drawn Colts in the back of Peg Dana as he prodded her along.

It was too incredible to absorb at first. "Smoking Jupiter," muttered Doc. When Red had hesitated, he thought it was the Law coming in as he saw Blair. But the sight of Peg, a captive, told him in a flash it was the law boss of Bridger, but he was not bringing the Law with him. Red guessed, correctly as he learned later that Peg, fretting for them, had ridden into town and told Blair how they were going to Crosby. Blair had come. But instinct told the outlaw's son now who was the power behind the evil thing that throttled Bridger.

Dornan didn't savvy it at first. "Why, Sheriff, we're just trying to bust –"

"Shut up!" barked the implacable-faced Blair at the word "Sheriff". "Come down off those steps! Hands up! Go get their guns," he barked to his men.

They had to obey. Doc stepped down first. They were just lifting out Doc's hoglegs. A man stepped around him to get at Dornan.

And Red Paine caught Peg's eyes. He read right away what he saw there; he knew they were doomed anyway. They could not be allowed to live – not out loose, anyway – after what they had learned. And that included the girl.

Red looked into her eyes. And he accepted the command. She would rather be killed than fail now. Stepping off the last step, Red pretended to stumble slightly.

"Get Molly ready," he whispered to Doc.

And then there was that draw akin to something like the stab of forked lightning. The guns whipping up with inhuman speed, a speed that could scarcely be followed by human eyes. And, with all the steel in him, he took the gamble. Even as Molly, Doc's beloved little club, came out of Doc's belt and whipped for the skull of that gunman, disarming them, Red shot. He shot at the head of the snake behind Peg, the one who had her spitted on his weapon. Red Paine shot that man dead through the brain before he could even cock a hammer.

Red had a fleeting glimpse of the girl flinging herself sideways and to cover by the corner of a barroom down there. Then the showdown battle was on. Dornan was on one knee in the grass beside the house, hammering away with both weapons. Roaring like a delighted bull, big Doc had snatched back his Colts from the man he'd slugged and had them talking. Red, leaping from the step, cut down one of the gents at the house corner. When he got to it, the other was diving away into the darkness at the rear. Red whirled and threw down with his weapons.

The turn in the tide of events was so sudden it was effective. Blair gunmen sank on all sides. Red zigzagged out into the middle of the alley. But then a handful of riders, who'd been waiting up on the main road, came pounding down. It looked like too much for the cornered trio.

Suddenly one of the horseman screeched with the agony of a wound, tried to twist in the kak. Another glanced behind. And in the misty yellow of the newborn day, Jud Tentrus came slamming down behind the horsemen, his big Colts spurting a vicious stream.

A slug whined by Red's chin. He saw Blair, his white shirt front making him stand out plainly, up there beside a little store. Then Blair disappeared down beside it. Right toward the horseman still headed down the lane, Red ran heedlessly. At last, Fate had given him his chance. Now he could settle the score with this lawman, the onetime Twin Forks deputy who had slain his father for a crime he hadn't committed; this lawman who himself had now gone bad.

Red dived into the narrow passageway beside the store. The red fang of a gun bit at him from the back. Bent low, he kept going. When he got into the rear, he saw something edge out in the grayness from behind a big crate. Red went flat. The bullet passed over him. Coming part way up, he fired as he saw Adam Blair dart from the other side of the crate on his short legs. Red, with his gun wizardry, could have killed that man then. Something held him back. He hit him in the leg.

It was just a flesh rip, sending Blair careening for a moment but not dropping him. Red was up and running. Blair veered eastward toward the bow of the creek, swung around a shed. Red began to zigzag. A bullet hit him high up in the flesh of the left shoulder, half spinning him. He got himself straight and went on, implacable, a manstalker. He swung out in an arc to get at the rear of the shed. It almost cost him his life.

Adam Blair, unseen, had backed away from it, was behind a clump of brush some yards from it. He came up into sight to fire. And Red Paine, with those inhuman reflexes, spotted him in time. Half twisting, he shot again. Again he could have killed the man perhaps. Blair's hat was gone and his head was plain. Blair did stumble backward, howling once. But the bullet had smashed his right arm as Red had intended.

Blair backed into a floating shed of the ground mist that had begun to boil up as the sun peeked over the eastern horizon. Then he seemed to drop from sight. Cutting to his left as he advanced, Red saw what it was, the bed of a dried-up feeder stream running down to the creek, almost hidden in the brush that fringed its little banks. Red dropped into it and stalked ahead, knowing he might be stalking to his death. Blair had the advantage now, even though limping, as he backed around the turns and bends.

One slug fanned Red's cheek. He offered no return fire. He kept going along the bed. Blair's left hand pushed from a clump of brush. Red shot and Blair beat a retreat without firing. They were almost at the creek. Red saw Blair trying to scramble up on the low banks. He fired, Blair rolled out of sight above with a bullet wound in his side. Red jumped up there. Ten feet away, sitting by a small rock, Adam Blair was hooking a derringer from his pocket. The Bridger sheriff started to twist it against his own body.

Though he knew he could be killed by the same gun at close range, Red Paine leaped in, for he knew the fate he had determined upon for the murder of his father. He leaped in and kicked; the derringer flew from Adam Blair's grasp a split second before it exploded harmlessly.

Red grabbed the man by the collar, hauled him onto his hind legs, and gave him a boot in the pants. "Go on, Blair! March! Drag yourself back – back to Bridger and the hangrope! That's how you're going to die, Adam Blair! To pay for my dad, Big Red Paine! You're going to stand trial – and be sentenced to hang like a common outlaw – and it'll be too good for you!"

He began to boot the limping man up the hill, laughing a little.

"Red! Red!" They were calling him up there. Only then did he realize the fight was over. Tentrus, slashing in from the rear, had turned the tide.

He shoved Adam Blair into the alley and they moved up it. Doc and Dornan came running down to meet him. Up beyond them he could see Blair's gun snakes who weren' dead or hadn't fled, standing before Redeye Jim's, hands hoisted, fronted by a scowling Tentrus.

"Red. . . . Oh, Red . . ." It was a little gasping sound. Then Peg Dana swirled from the shadows and into his arms. It was the first time he kissed her. He did it in plain sight of everybody – and did it again and again.

CHAPTER TWENTY-ONE

Tentrus explained how he'd happened in. He did it with an apology to Red. "I guess – well, I reckon I didn't quite trust you. . . . Er, mebbe it was I hate to admit it to gents of – well, of your breed – that a lawman could go wrong. . . . Sunday night, when Robles was killed in jail, I was scouting around as usual. I was near that mound behind the jailhouse. . . . Nobody shot Robles from there. He – he was shot inside the jailhouse. And Adam Blair," he spat toward the wounded man huddled on the steps, looking like a bag, "was the only one in the jail at the time. . . . After that, I kept watch on him, waiting for him to show his hand. Last night, when he took off and met these gun scum outside town, I trailed 'em down here. Then –" He said the rest with an expressive shrug.

Tentrus took over command for a few minutes. He picked out two men he knew had been in the Vigilantes before he'd left Bridger to become a U.S. marshal. It didn't

211

take more than a few minutes of Tentrus' forceful methods before they were confessing to save their own necks.

Actually, it was very simple. Some of the Vigilantes had turned bad, then hooked up with Law itself in the form of ambitious Adam Blair. Others had been dropped from the organization. Gunmen had been brought into it; that was why the roster had been kept secret, with nobody knowing who was a Vigilante. And a great gang had been welded to rule Bridger, to rob and kill and stage holdups with impunity.

One of the confessing men turned to curse at Adam Blair. Red, with the sunshine streaming into the alley, got a good look at the prisoner behind him. And Red Paine's heart leaped. It was the duded-up Powell, still in the fancy silk shirt, the man with the cast in his eye whom he was supposed to have helped escape from the Red Hat jail. Now Red, knew, squeezing the waist of the girl who stood beside him a little bit tighter, that when they got back to Bridger he would be cleared at last. He would have no charge against him. . . .

It was a little later when in broad daylight they rode out across the flats to Riley's Castle. Blair had been bandaged up and was in the

van with a gun in his back. They came to the gates of the walled-in great dobie Mexican-style hacienda that everybody thought stood crumbling and empty out there. Blair called out and identified himself. At his order, half a dozen gunmen came out. They were easily taken, only one of them putting up a fight. Dornan dropped him with a slug in the leg.

Tentrus, with a surprising show of sensitivity, said something to Red. He kept the girl outside. Some of the others went in. Some minutes passed. Strange bleating sounds came from the bowels of the place. And then the strange procession began.

Tottering with weakness, half-starved, helped up from the great bowel-like cellars of the place men began to come slowly. Prematurely white-haired. Shielding their eyes against the sudden sunlight with clawlike hands. Some of them showing the signs of beatings. They pushed feebly out onto the porch, staggered down the stairs to drop onto the ground. Some of them wept tears of joy.

Dornan pointed out a man a few degrees removed from a skeleton. "Hop Malady," he identified him somehow. "U.S. marshal. Used to be a big two-hundred pound bull, too."

213

It was a pitiful sight, these men coming back from a living death, these men who had stumbled on Adam Blair's secret, who had learned something in Bridger City. And they had been put away as hostages to rot slowly while their families were drained of blood and money for ransom to keep them from dying, while the very fact they lived was used as a club over those who came to try to avenge them. Then Peg Dana gave a choked little cry. She ran forward to help a tall, distinguished-looking man down the steps. Red knew it was her father, Matt Dana. He watched the old man stare, not recognizing her at first. Then they were clutched in each other's arms.

Red turned away. He could see the dust of a rider, a man of Crosby, as he galloped across the flats, headed for Bridger. Tentrus had sent him to have the citizens' committee, the group that had hired him to come back, send out some dependable men to help bring in the prisoners as well as these crippled wretches released from a living death.

There was a firmer step near Red. A voice said, "You wouldn't be Little Red Paine, would you?"

Red turned to face one of the released men, a much younger one, standing there in

tattered rags of clothes, half hidden beneath a head of beard. There was something familiar about the blond beard and hair above it.

"Isn't it incredible, John Hugo?" said another of the stumbling men fresh from the cellar of Riley's castle. There were tears in his eyes even as he laughed weakly.

"Yes, I'm Red Paine," Red said to the man named John Hugo.

"The man who got us out – from what I hear," said the other. Then he was cursing, seizing Red by the shoulders and shaking him. "You fool kid! I always knew you were the smartest one of us, the best one! I'm Hugo – Hugo Paine, Red – your brother!" He choked up a moment. "I was captured when I came down to Bridger after a man in line of duty."

"Hugo?" Red gasped, hardly able to believe it.

"Sure. Red, I'm the town marshal in a pueblo called Sweetgrass Forks. Had to change my name – you can see why. Red, you sure look fine!" He laughed crazily.

"Hugo!" Red hugged the half-hysterical brother he had believed lost forever. "Hugo – a John Law! I'll be danged!" He looked skyward, sort of nodded, thinking of his dad.

He would have liked this.

Then, over Hugo's shoulder, he saw big Jud Tentrus coming down from the veranda of the place, coming directly toward him. Red stepped back, the stony shine coming into his eyes. Now that the big job was done, he had that score to settle with Tentrus. The latter halted a couple of feet from Red, his face a hard mask.

"Paine, after what I saw you do here – and before in this deal – I've learned something," Tentrus said slowly. "I've come to realize that no matter what he might have been by accident of Fate, your father must've been a heck of a fine man. Fast ponies don't come from slow mares. Your father, Big Red, must've been strong to breed one as strong as you." He cleared his throat. "You gave me back my hoglegs so we could do this job. Now – it's done." Slowly he drew out his hardware and extended it to Red Paine, butts foremost.

Red hesitated. The old hating antipathy for this ruthless man lashed up in him. Then something else began to replace it. Though a full head shorter than the big John Law, he felt bigger in that moment as he smiled slightly and shook his head to refuse the extended weapons.

"You two ought to know each other," Red

said, taking his brother's arm, "being in the same business. Hugo here is a lawman too, Tentrus. Hugo is a son of my father, too. . . ."

4-8-09

5\92

BOOT HILL

WITHDRAWN

Weston Clay

When Red Paine's father died a violent death at the hands of a vengeful posse, he fled to a strange country to start life anew amongst people who had never heard his father's name. But the outlaw brand traveled faster and farther and young Red grew to manhood on the dodge . . . until there was no ~~~ go, no place to hide . . . when course left to him was to fight take the same road his father h – a one-way road to an unmark in Boot Hill!